Look for:

Indigo Summer
by Monica McKayhan
ISBN-13: 978-0-373-83075-6
ISBN-10: 0-373-83075-0

Can't Stop the Shine
by Joyce E. Davis
ISBN-13: 978-0-373-83078-7
ISBN-10: 0-373-83078-5

Keysha's Drama
by Earl Sewell
ISBN-13: 978-0-373-83079-4
ISBN-10: 0-373-83079-3

www.KimaniTRU.com

spin it like that

CHANDRA
SPARKS TAYLOR

SPIN IT LIKE THAT

ISBN-13: 978-0-373-83080-0
ISBN-10:   0-373-83080-7

www.KimaniTRU.com

Printed in U.S.A.

FRESH. CURRENT. AND TRUE TO YOU

Dear Reader,

What you're holding is very special and unique. Something fresh, new and in the mix! We are proud to introduce a new fiction imprint...Kimani TRU. An exceptional line of novels especially written *for* African-American young adults and will spotlight young, emerging literary talent. You'll find Kimani TRU addresses the triumphs, issues and concerns of today's black teens with candor, wit and realism. From your perspective and in your own voice.

Crafted specifically with the tastes and interests of your generation in mind, Kimani TRU novels will reflect the coming-of-age obstacles you face in today's fast-paced world, with compelling prose, realistic dialogue, and jam-packed with references and cultural icons that are so much a part of your life.

Kimani TRU is an imprint proud to feature stories that are down-to-earth, yet also empowering. Feeling like an outsider? Afraid you'll never have a cool boyfriend or that your life is a disaster on the fast track to nowhere? Discover in Kimani TRU novels emotional issues that characters will face. One young man battles to get out of Oakland to attend a historically black college. In another story, a young woman's life drastically changes after her father remarries and they move to the suburbs. And in still another, two sisters forge different paths after secrets about their lives are revealed.

Kimani TRU. Novels that provide a rare and unique voice and will appeal to *all* readers of your generation! Our goal is to touch your heart, mind and soul by allowing you to express your creativity and your literary voice.

Spread the word…Kimani TRU. True to you!

Linda Gill
General Manager
Kimani Press

 KIMANI PRESS™

To my parents, the late Cedric Louis Sparks and the late Doris Jones Sparks. I hope I've made you proud.

Acknowledgments

First and foremost, I have to give honor to God, who during the most tumultuous time in my life has blessed me to fulfill my lifelong dream. He has truly given me beauty from the ashes. Thank you so much for all your many blessings. I love you with all my heart, and I pray that my words make you proud and help me on my journey to be the voice of the next generation.

To Curtis and Jamaal Taylor. Thank you for allowing me to be a part of your lives. May God bless you so much you don't have room to receive it all. Please know that I love you both.

To my beautiful brown-eyed girl, Jessica Taylor. It is because of you that I have fulfilled my lifelong dream. Never forget how much your mommy loves you, my sweet baby girl. Never be afraid to dream.

To my parents, the late Cedric Louis Sparks and the late Doris Jones Sparks, thank you for instilling in me a love for God and the enjoyment of reading. I love you and I miss you.

To my supersupportive family: my brothers, Andra and Cedric Sparks; my sisters-in-law, Karen and Pamela Sparks; my incredible nieces and nephews, Anthony, Brittany, CJ and DeJa; and my uncle Edward Lamonte Johnson. I love you all more than words can say. P.S. Where are we going to eat to celebrate?

To the rest of my extended family: my grandparents, George and Lela Jones and the late Ida B. Sparks; my great-aunt Rosie Mae O'Bryant; my aunts Carolyn Hollman, Geraldine Murray, the late Minnie Jones Ford, Janice Jones, Cynthia Sparks and Deborah Sparks; my uncles George Jones, Jr., Robert Jones, Sr., David Jones, Sr., Tommy Jones, Sr., Michael Jones, Sr., the late Hosiea V. Sparks, Sr., and Lasco Sparks; Charles Murray and Reverend Larry Hollman; as well as all my cousins, especially Tiffany Murray Simmons, Charles Renard Murray, DeRenda Hollman and Arianna Johnson; and my dog, Rex. I love you.

Acknowledgment (cont'd)

To my girls for life: Allilsa Bradley, Toni Staton Harris, Nancey Flowers, Adrianne Durr Caldwell, Shandra Hill and Jacquelin Thomas, as well as my new friends Darlene Powell-Garlington, LaConnie Taylor-Jones, Na Toya Payne, Dana Olmsted, Francine Craft, Leslie Esdaile, Celeste Norfleet and Kathy Lee. Thank you, ladies, for always having my back and for teaching me more about God and his love. I'd also like to acknowledge the friends who came into my life for a reason or a season. Thank you for the lessons you taught me.

To my editor, Glenda Howard, as well as Linda Gill and the staff of Kimani Press. Thank you for believing in me enough to publish my work. I pray we have a long and prosperous relationship.

I've been blessed to have a dynamic support system across the country. I would be remiss if I didn't thank the members of the First Missionary Baptist Church, East Boyles, in Tarrant, Alabama; Shiloh Baptist Church in Jamaica, New York, especially Pastor Russell Marquis and his wife, Martrice; Forty-fifth Street Baptist Church in Birmingham; the Queens chapter of Mocha Moms, Inc.; Alpha Kappa Alpha Sorority, Inc., especially the Theta Sigma chapter (What's up, T.I.P. and F^3?) and the Epsilon Pi Omega chapter; Ramsay Alternative High School in Birmingham; the University of Alabama at Tuscaloosa; and the Richardsons— Clem, Claudette, Marien and Jené.

I also have to acknowledge my editing clients over the years. Thank you for allowing me to serve you. It is my sincere hope that you have been pleased with my work.

Finally, to anyone who does me the honor of reading this novel, I have to say thank you. I pray that my words help you on your journey to becoming all that God wants you to be and that we'll meet again soon.

God bless you,
Chandra Sparks Taylor

chapter 1

Sweat popped off me and my heart danced as I scratched out beats until my fingers burned. I hunched my back so I was closer to my mixing board and bopped my head to the beat, waiting for my cue to start my solo, as my brother, Derrick Richardson, worked the crowd, spitting unrehearsed rhymes off the top of his head.

The audience was on fire, and so were we.

When I started my solo, my body took over, and I started vibing with the music. I no longer felt the pain in my fingers, and my face was so close to the vinyl that I could almost kiss it as I focused on making that record sing a new song. It was like I was outside myself, watching as I did these crazy combinations that had the crowd on their feet yelling my stage name, Jazzy J, and grooving to my beats. Their energy was unlike anything I had ever known in all my sixteen years, and I lived for it.

Derrick took center stage again, and I harmonized with him before belting out a few lines from an R & B tune that would put Mary J. Blige to shame. The crowd was in awe. Most people knew I could deejay, but they had no clue that I was a fierce singer, and I could rap, too. I had been saving my singing for the perfect moment, and that time was now— during the biggest performance of our lives. When Derrick was done, I scratched one last beat, then came from behind my Technics 1200 turntable and grabbed his hand. We took a bow as the crowd whistled and shouted so loud my ears hurt.

We were the final act for the All-District Rap Invitational, which had gathered the top acts from Queens, New York, to compete for a spot in All-City. There, the winner from each of the city's boroughs—Manhattan, Brooklyn, Queens, Staten Island and the Bronx—would battle for a deal with Impact Records, a company that was known for producing hits. Derrick and I were favorites to win All-District, and as far as I was concerned, All-District and All-City were just formalities. That record contract already had my name on it.

Derrick leaned over, sweat streaming down his

chocolate-brown face, and gave me a high five. "Good job, Jasmine," he yelled, sounding a little hoarse.

"Thanks." I grinned at him as I whipped a towel from around my neck and handed it to him. "I knew you'd forget to bring one."

He smiled his thanks as he wiped his face, then threw the towel into the crowd. The girls went crazy as they fought to get it, and I couldn't help but laugh as Derrick blushed. He didn't like the spotlight at all, although he was an incredible rapper.

I watched as the other participants took the stage, and I tried to keep from laughing when I spotted the group that had come on before us. They had forgotten half their routine and had walked off the stage in disgrace after the crowd started booing them. I was surprised they had the nerve to show their faces again. I know if it had been me... Nah, that would never be me. My routine was always tight.

The MC finally made his way to the stage again, and he told a few corny jokes while the judges tabulated our scores. I figured they were just doing it for show, because there was no doubt in my mind that Derrick and I had won.

When the third-place winner was announced, I smiled at my brother. They had been good, as had a few of the nineteen acts besides us, and even though I knew we were the best, I was still anxious about actually hearing our name called. When a solo performer was named the second-place winner, I didn't know whether to be happy or nervous. I crossed the fingers of my right hand behind my back and bounced in place, probably looking like I had to pee, as I silently encouraged the MC to call our names, and Derrick squeezed my other hand to calm me down.

"We want to thank all our acts for performing tonight," the MC said, "and now without further ado, the winner of the first annual All-District Rap Invitational is Jazzy J and Kid D."

The roar of the crowd was so loud that I could hardly hear who had won. It wasn't until Derrick lifted me up and spun me around that I realized it was us.

"We did it," he shouted.

"We did it?" I repeated, making sure I hadn't heard him wrong.

He nodded as he put me down, smiling so hard I thought his face was gonna split in two. We walked over to the announcer and accepted our trophy and a check for a thousand dollars; then we waved to the crowd, which continued to cheer for us.

I spotted my friends Kyle Adams and Loretta Dennis in the front row, and they looked just as excited as I felt. I pointed to the trophy and grinned. Like my brother, my friends knew just how much I wanted to win this contest. It had always been my dream to land a record deal, and now I was one step closer.

Life just couldn't get any better.

"Nice show," a man said as I pushed through the crowd to head offstage to meet my friends. It seemed like everybody and their mama had decided to come onstage to congratulate us, and it looked like it would take me a good twenty minutes to make my way to Kyle and Loretta.

"Thanks," I said, showing off my perfect white teeth once again. I looked at the trophy to make sure it was still there and that I wasn't dreaming; then I glanced back at the guy as I pushed a lock of my curly hair out of my face. It was so hot in the Springfield Auditorium in Queens that my sandy-colored hair had become frizzy and had worked its way out of its ponytail. The man was big and dark, and he kind of reminded me of Big Rick from *Flavor of Love,* except he had a huge purple wide-brimmed hat that matched his purple shirt, which he wore with a white three-piece suit and a white tie. The fumes from his cigar mixed with the funk of the auditorium had me about to choke. I sniffed politely, but it didn't help.

When he blew another puff of smoke my way, I got annoyed.

"Don't you see the no-smoking signs in here?" I said, pointing to one above his head. "If you want to kill yourself, fine, but I'm too young to die."

He grinned at me and blew smoke in my direction, which really made me mad. I rolled my eyes and smacked my lips before turning to walk off.

"Do you play at parties and clubs?" he asked.

"Sure," I said, turning to look at him again. I caught a glimpse of Loretta over the guy's shoulder. She was saying something, but she was too far away for me to hear her. I shrugged and looked at the guy again. "My brother and I have performed all over Queens."

He nodded and stuck his cigar in his mouth again before he flicked a business card from his wallet. "Why don't you give my assistant a call? I might have some work for you."

"Have your assistant call me," I said.

He gave this deep laugh, and his whole frame shook. "You're a spunky little thing. I like that," he said, and grinned. "Call my assistant," he insisted.

"Okay," I said, taking the card. I got numbers all the time from people who said they wanted me to play at their parties, but most of them never ended up following through. "Nice meeting you," I said, not bothering to look at him as I headed over to my friends.

"We won," I said, giving both Kyle and Loretta a hug.

"Congratulations," Kyle said, giving me a pound and slinging his arm around my shoulder. "That show was hot."

I turned to Loretta, but she was looking past me. I turned to see what she was staring at, but no one was there. "Hey," I said, tapping her on the shoulder. "You're not gon' congratulate me?"

"Do you know who that was?" she asked, continuing to look past me.

"Who?" I asked.

Loretta finally focused on me and smiled like she had just seen her future baby daddy. "That was Dexter Chamberlain," she said, smoothing her hair.

"Who's that?" I asked, wrinkling my nose. The name sounded familiar, but I couldn't remember where I had heard it.

"That dude from DC Records," Kyle said, and shrugged.

DC Records had been around for years, and the company had a huge stable of chart-topping gangsta rappers.

"You mean DC Chamberlain?" I asked as my eyes got wide. "I didn't know his first name was Dexter."

Loretta nodded. "What did he want?"

"He told me he might have some work for me."

"He probably wants to sign you," Loretta said, getting excited. "I think I heard somewhere he wants to move away from gangsta rap." She jumped up and down and pulled on my shoulder. "You'd be perfect. When you get a deal, can I be on the cover of your first CD?"

Loretta was desperate to break into the modeling game, but somehow none of her gigs ever came through.

"Sure," I said, and laughed as Derrick walked up.

I filled him in on my encounter with DC Chamberlain, and he looked almost as unimpressed as Kyle.

"Do you really think he's interested in signing us?" I asked, trying not to show my excitement.

Kyle frowned. "If he is, you better run in the other direction. I know you've heard about that man's reputation."

Derrick nodded.

I looked at Loretta, and I could see she was already picturing herself in my first video, too. "What do you care about his reputation as long as you get your name out there?" She shrugged and glanced away before pouting her lips, smoothing her weave and looking over her shoulder, posing for a *Daily News* photographer who had come over to take our picture.

I thought about what Loretta had said, and I realized she was right. Obviously DC knew I had skills or he wouldn't have asked me to call him. If I had his support, there was no way I could lose All-City.

chapter 2

By the time Derrick and I made it back to Hollis, it was almost two o'clock in the morning, and we had missed our midnight curfew. Derrick had wanted to head home as soon as the competition was over, but I had convinced him that we needed to go out and celebrate. I knew we would be late, but I figured my daddy would be so excited we'd won that he'd talk to Mama so she wouldn't be upset. Since I knew we were going to be in trouble, I hadn't bothered to call, and I wouldn't give Derrick his phone so he could call.

After we'd dropped Loretta and Kyle off, I drove with the radio booming, until Derrick made me turn down the volume.

"Man, I didn't think Loretta was ever gon' stop talking about her picture being in the paper," I said when the quiet finally started getting to me. "I hope that girl lands a deal soon. She's about to drive me crazy talking about modeling."

"That's all she talks about," Derrick agreed, looking out his window.

"Yeah, that's true. It's cool that we're gonna be in the paper, though, huh?" I said, tapping my fingers against the steering wheel.

"You think they're still up?" Derrick asked, ignoring me as we got off the Cross Island Parkway at the Hempstead Turnpike exit. We had headed to a local diner for something to eat before dropping off Kyle and Loretta, who both lived in Rosedale.

"Who knows?" I said, shrugging. I took my eyes off the road and briefly glanced at him. "So what, we're a little late. We're not gon' let them ruin this night for us, okay?"

Derrick tried to look as though he wasn't worried, but I knew he was, so I changed the subject.

"Man, where did you come up with those lyrics? That's not what we rehearsed."

Derrick shrugged and grinned sheepishly. He was really shy except when he was around people he was close to and when he got onstage. Then he became a different person. "You know how it is when the music takes over," he said.

I did know. I loved the way working the crowd made me feel.

"That note you hit was crazy." He looked at me and raised an eyebrow, still amazed at my vocal talent.

"Yeah, you know I've got skills." I grinned.

We listened to the radio for a couple of blocks, and I felt him starting to worry again.

"When are you gonna get that clunker of yours fixed? I'm tired of chauffeuring you around," I joked. Truthfully, although Derrick was two years older than me, we were as close as twins, but we looked totally different. We were like a Reese's candy cup: his skin was the color of milk chocolate, and mine was like peanut butter. We did everything together, and I liked hanging with him. We were both graduating from high school the next week, and we would be freshmen at Morgan State in the fall—he was going to major in biology, and I was thinking about music, but I hadn't made up my mind.

I had skipped ninth grade, so Derrick and I were both graduating from Queens Academy that Thursday. We were covaledictorians, so we each had to give a speech. Derrick had been working on his for weeks, but I hadn't even started mine.

Derrick laughed. Thanks to the local performances at parties we had been doing for the last two years, we had created a buzz for ourselves in Queens, and with the money we'd made, we had both been able to buy used cars. I had gotten my Honda Civic a few months earlier for my sixteenth birthday. Derrick had gotten an old Honda Prelude. It stayed in the shop more than it did on the road, but he loved his car as much as I did mine.

"What are you gonna buy with the prize money?" I asked.

Derrick pushed back his baseball cap and rubbed his hand over his close-cropped hair as he thought. "I don't know," he finally said. "I still can't believe we won." He looked down at the trophy, which he held between his legs, probably to make sure it was still there. "What about you?"

"Maybe that leather jacket I saw at that store on Jamaica Ave.," I said.

"Yeah, it was nice," Derrick said, and stroked his chin. "But maybe you should wait. Summer is about to start."

We had seen the black full-length coat when we had gone to look for turntable equipment a few weeks ago, and I hadn't been able to get it out of my head.

"Yeah, you're right. Maybe I'll just save my half of the money and treat myself to the coat when we land our deal."

"You really think we're going to win All-City?"

I took my eyes off the road for a second to look at him. "I know we are," I said. "I mean, some of those acts were good, but they weren't as good as us. We'll just practice every chance we get between now and August. Don't forget they still don't know I can rap."

He nodded thoughtfully. We turned onto our block and saw that the living room light was on, as it usually was when we went out. Derrick glanced at me.

"They're probably asleep," I said. I tried to sound convincing, but I didn't think I pulled it off, since he looked at me real skeptical.

We walked in the door, and Mama looked like she had been in the same spot since we'd left earlier that evening.

"Do you know what time it is?" she asked, getting up to meet us at the front door. We didn't get a chance to answer. "I've called you half a dozen times."

"But Mama—" I said.

"Do I look like I need you to say anything right

now? Do you know how worried I've been?" She looked from Derrick to me, and I didn't know whether we should answer. "Do you hear me talking to you?" she asked through clenched teeth.

"But Mama, we won," I said, grabbing the trophy from Derrick and holding it up for her to see. "We get to compete in All-City, and when we win, we'll get a record deal. We're gonna be famous."

Mama ignored me and turned to Derrick. "I know Jasmine put you up to this. You know better than to be out this late without calling me. What has gotten into you?"

Derrick looked at the floor in silence, and I immediately jumped to his defense. "Mama, it was my fault. I wanted to go out to celebrate. My cell phone battery was dead, and I had Derrick's phone in my purse, which is why we didn't get your messages."

She looked at me like she didn't believe a word I was saying.

"For real, Mama. Look, I promise it won't happen again—"

"I know it won't," Mama said. "The two of you are grounded for the rest of the summer."

"What?" I screamed. I couldn't believe she was being so unfair. It wasn't like we missed curfew that often. "But Mama, didn't you hear me? We're going to All-City. We have to practice, and we have all those parties lined up. Please, we'll do anything you ask, but you can't put us on punishment now."

Mama walked toward the back of the house, indicating that we weren't going to talk about it anymore. I glanced at Derrick, and he just stood there. I ran to catch up with her. "Mama, you can't do this!" I yelled, trying to keep from crying.

All our screaming woke Daddy, who stood in the door of their bedroom, rubbing his eyes. "What's going on?" he asked sleepily.

"You need to talk to your daughter," Mama said, turning to look at me.

Whenever I did anything wrong, she didn't claim me.

I ran over to him. "Daddy, we won," I said, showing him the trophy.

His eyes lit up. "Congratulations, baby," he said. He picked me up and spun me around, placing a kiss on my cheek. Mama frowned. "Oh, come on, baby," he said, looking at her. "That's great news."

"Daddy, I didn't tell you the best part of all: we get to go to All-City, and when we win there, we get a record deal!" I screamed. I jumped around as the reality of my words set in.

Mama and Daddy never attended any of our performances. I think they reminded Daddy too much of his past and all he had given up. He had just been about to sign a record deal when Mama told him she was pregnant with Derrick. They'd both had to drop out of school and get jobs to take care of Derrick and then me when I came along two years later. Although they never said they regretted not finishing college, I always wondered if they did. They were constantly riding Derrick and me about the importance of getting our education, making sure to mention that my cousins were doing well in college, and all the talk was starting to get on my nerves.

Derrick and I had gotten to the point where we stopped talking to them about our performances, because my parents—especially my mother—always managed to work education into the conversation.

I had totally tuned Daddy out, and when I refocused on the conversation, Derrick had come into the hall and Mama was once again going on about the importance of education.

"You're starting college in a couple of months, and since you'll be on punishment for the rest of the summer, you can just tell whoever that you won't be performing in that competition, so there won't be a record deal."

"Mama!" Derrick and I both shouted. I knew he probably was more upset for me than for himself. Although Derrick liked music, it was really my dream to pursue it professionally, not his.

I turned to Daddy. "Daddy, please don't let her do this," I whined.

Mama ignored me. "As long as you're living in my house, you're going to abide by my rules," she said.

"Daddy," I wailed again.

"Don't bring your father into this," Mama said, giving Daddy that look that parents exchange. "I've made my decision, and that's final." She turned to go into her room, which meant the conversation was over.

I looked at Daddy, silently pleading with him to talk to her. "I'm sorry, baby," he said. He had learned from experience not to get into our arguments.

"This isn't fair," I whined.

Mama spun around. "I've had just about enough of you, young lady." She looked like she had a lot more to say, but I didn't want to hear it.

"No, I'm the one who's had enough," I yelled.

My outburst shocked everyone into silence. I couldn't believe I had actually let the words out. I mean, I had thought them plenty of times, but I liked my life too much to say them out loud.

"You're always trying to run my life. I'm sick of it. You're not going to ruin this chance for us. I'll move out if I have to," I said, and flew to the safety of my room.

I was relieved when I woke up around nine the next morning to find that Mama and Daddy had already left for work. My daddy, Thomas Richardson, drove the Q4 bus route in Cambria Heights, and my mama, Patricia, worked at the post office in Laurelton. They both seemed to like their jobs just fine—until my uncle Henry came around. Uncle Henry is a year younger than Daddy, and he owned some big-time law firm in Manhattan. He and Daddy didn't talk much, because Daddy said Uncle Henry only knew two things to talk about—the past and his kids.

Daddy said he and Uncle Henry were supposed to be as big as some of the old-school rappers—Uncle Henry was going to be the rapper, Daddy was the DJ and some guy named Chubby was going to be the producer. They used to hang out with a lot of famous people before those people were stars and everything, since they all grew up in the same neighborhood. We lived in the house Daddy and Uncle Henry had grown up in, another thing Uncle Henry never let Daddy forget.

Apparently, Uncle Henry was still mad that Daddy messed up their future. I always wondered why Uncle Henry just didn't go through with his plans on his own. Once I had asked Daddy, but he'd told me to stay out of grown folks' business, so I never brought it up again, but I wondered just the same. Derrick said he thought Uncle Henry dropped it because he wasn't as passionate as Daddy, sort of like me and Derrick. Music was okay for Derrick, but for me it was like breathing.

I headed to the kitchen, grabbed a bowl of cereal and flopped down in a chair. I thought about turning on the TV, but I wasn't in the mood, so I flipped through the copy of the *Daily News* that Daddy had left on the table. Our picture had made it into the paper. I knew Loretta was gonna be mad, because she and Kyle had been cut out. If I looked real close, I could see her shoulder.

I shook my head as Derrick walked in.

"Hey," he said. "What are you looking at?"

I showed him the picture, and he started laughing. "Dang, that girl just can't get a break," he said.

Loretta was always trying to get her big break as a model, but nothing ever seemed to work out for her. I thought it had something to do with her body. Although she was only sixteen, she had the full butt and hips of a grown woman. She was almost too shapely for modeling. And she had gotten scammed out of so much money it was crazy, but that didn't stop her from pursuing her dream, which I could understand.

Derrick grabbed a bowl and poured some cereal. "Do you think Mama's going to keep us on lockdown for the rest of the summer?"

I shrugged, and we ate in silence for a while until I couldn't take it anymore. I turned on the television, and we watched a few videos. When one of DC Records' artists came on, I remembered the card I had gotten from Dexter Chamberlain the night before, and tried to remember where I had put it.

"It's in your car," Derrick said without looking at me.

"How do you know what I'm thinking?" I asked.

He didn't bother to respond to my question. "Am I wrong?"

"No," I said with an attitude. He drove me crazy when he knew what I was thinking, sometimes before I even knew. I headed out to my car and searched until I spotted the business card on the floor of the passenger seat. I had given it to Derrick the night before because I was known to lose stuff.

"Should I call him?" I asked nervously when I

returned to the kitchen. Derrick exhaled in disgust. "I guess that was a stupid question," I said, picking up the cordless phone.

I chewed on a nail as I waited for someone to pick up on the other end. I was just about to hang up when I heard a bored-sounding voice say, "Thank you for calling DC Records. How may I help you?"

I took a deep breath. I had never called a record company before, so I didn't know what to expect. "Hi, my name is Jasmine Richardson. Mr. Chamberlain asked me to call him today."

The woman on the other end brightened. "Oh, hi. I'm Jessica, DC's assistant. I've been expecting your call."

"You have?" I asked nervously.

"Yes. Are you familiar with Teen Scene?"

"No. What's that?" I asked. Derrick looked at me, silently asking me what she had said, but I held up a finger to let him know I'd tell him in a minute.

"It's something DC decided to start a few months ago. He wants to turn a local club into a hangout for teens where they can dance and have fun in a drug- and alcohol-free environment. We're going to do a test run in Queens before we expand. The parties are going to be held every week starting in two weeks until the end of the summer."

"Oh, that's pretty cool," I said, wondering what this had to do with me. I looked at Derrick and shrugged before waving my hand to try and make Jessica to get to the point.

"Our DJ canceled on us last week…" At that, I sat up straight.

"Really?" I said.

"DC wants to hire you to play the parties."

"Okay," I quickly said.

Jessica laughed. "You don't know any of the details yet."

"Oh." I tried to calm down when I realized just how immature and unprofessional I sounded. I didn't want to talk myself out of a job.

"I have a contract I use," I said, hoping this made me sound more businesslike.

"That's fine," Jessica said. "I'll send you a copy of our contract, and you can send yours back with it. The parties will last from eight until midnight, and they'll be held at Twilight on Linden Boulevard in St. Albans."

"That's not too far from me," I said, recalling the club. It had been around a long time, but lately it seemed that there was always something going on there. I had heard advertisements for karaoke and comedy nights. Whenever Derrick and I drove past on weekends, there was always a huge crowd waiting to get in.

Derrick was staring at me again, and I smiled at him.

"You'll be performing Thursday and Friday nights. You'll need to be there no later than seven each evening, and you'll be paid a thousand dollars a week."

"A thousand dollars a week?" I said slowly, and Derrick raised an eyebrow.

"Is that okay?" Jessica asked.

I sighed, pretending I had to think it over. "I guess so," I said. I tried not to let my excitement show in my voice, although I was tapping Derrick on the arm. I had never made that much for working an event, and I couldn't believe I'd be making it every week. It looked like I wouldn't have to wait until I landed my record deal to get my leather coat. "Are we supposed to split that?" I asked in my most professional voice.

"We?" Jessica asked, sounding confused.

"Yeah, me and my brother, Derrick. We're a team," I said.

Jessica hesitated. "DC didn't mention anything about your brother. I'll have to call him."

I looked at Derrick, who was shaking his head.

"Could you hold on for a minute?" I asked. I covered the phone with my hand, hoping Jessica wouldn't hear me. "What?"

"Take the job," he said.

"But I can't do it without you," I whispered.

"Jasmine, this is your dream, not mine," he said. "Take the job."

I didn't know what to do. I was used to Derrick being by my side when I performed. "Will you come with me?" I asked in a small voice, suddenly scared of the thought of being without him.

He nodded, and I felt a relief I couldn't describe. "Thank you," I said. I removed my hand from the receiver. "Jessica, don't worry about calling DC. I'll do the club by myself."

"Great," she said, sounding relieved. "This is a really great opportunity for you. A lot of rap's pioneers got their starts at the club, and DC has asked a lot of celebrities to drop by, so you should get some really good exposure."

I smiled as I envisioned myself hanging out with some of the people I watched in videos.

"Hello?" Jessica said.

I shook myself and refocused on the conversation. "Yes, I'm here," I said.

"I'll messenger our in-house contract to you

today," she said. "Sign it and get it back to us as soon as you can."

"Okay. Thank you," I said, and hung up. I looked at Derrick, who was smiling.

"Congratulations," he said, giving me a hug.

"Oh, man, wait until I tell Loretta and Kyle," I said. "Daddy is gonna be excited, too." I looked at Derrick, and his expression made me put down the phone. "What?" I asked.

Before he could respond, the back door opened, and in walked Mama.

chapter 3

"Good morning," Mama said, sounding tired. She didn't bother to look at me as she placed a few bags of groceries on the table, and I knew she was still mad, so I jumped up to put them away. Derrick got up to help, but I waved him off.

"Hey, Mama. What are you doing home?" I asked nervously as I remembered our argument from the night before.

"I decided to take the rest of the day off. It was kind of slow at work today, so I came on home. I was feeling fine until I stopped at the grocery store. Now my head is killing me." She rubbed her temples. "Our argument last night has my pressure up."

I continued to put away the groceries in silence. I was trying to think of a way to talk her into letting me perform at Twilight every week, since I was supposed to be on punishment for the rest of the summer.

"Do you need me to do anything else, Mama?" I asked once I was done.

"Could you get me a glass of water and some aspirin?" she said, settling into a seat at the kitchen table.

"Okay," I said, probably a bit too eagerly. I didn't want to give her any more reason to be angry with me.

She smiled her thanks when I came back with the aspirin. "What do you guys have planned for the day?" she asked.

Derrick and I looked at each other. "We have graduation practice later, and I need to work on my speech, but other than that, nothing. We were just going to hang around the house, maybe clean up," I threw in.

Mama stopped massaging her temples and looked at me. "What are you up to?" she asked suspiciously.

Derrick kicked me under the table, silently urging me to go ahead and tell Mama about the job offer. I chewed my lip, trying to decide if I should say something to her or wait for Daddy to come home, since I could talk him into just about anything.

The decision was made for me when Mama suddenly grabbed her head.

"Are you okay?" Derrick asked, going to check on her.

She tried to shake her head and winced. Derrick grabbed her arm and led her to her bedroom, where we both tucked her in like she used to do us when we were little kids. After making sure the shades were drawn and that Mama was comfortable, we got ready to go to practice.

"Why didn't you tell her?" Derrick asked on the way to school.

"You know she's just gonna say no," I said. "I'll wait until Daddy comes home. I know I can get him to say yes."

Derrick nodded and turned on the hip hop station. We were nodding to an old-school rap when the announcer broke in.

"We interrupt this program for a late-breaking announcement. Dexter 'DC' Chamberlain was arrested outside his Manhattan office today in connection with the murder of West Coast gangsta rapper Malik, who was killed two years ago."

Derrick and I looked at each other. I turned up the radio just as we pulled into the school parking lot.

"This is not the first time Chamberlain, who is the

founder of DC Records, has had a brush with authorities. He has launched the careers of several well-known gangsta rappers. We will bring you more details as they become available."

"Man, that's messed up," Derrick said, shaking his head.

"Yeah. Do you think they're still going to go through with the parties?"

"We'll see," Derrick said. He reached for the door handle and climbed out, but I didn't move. "It's going to be fine," he said through the window. "Even if this doesn't work out, it's not your last chance. You can still win the record deal with Impact."

I nodded. I was already starting to blow up, and although the gig with DC would generate more hype, I would be just fine without it. My skills spoke for themselves.

Impact Records had only been around a few years, but they had a great reputation. Kyle had told me that the guy who started it had once been DC's protégé, but he didn't like the gangsta rap and controversy that DC Records was known for, so he had started his own label. I had quite a few CDs by Impact artists, and all of them were good. Once Derrick and I won All-City, we would be a great addition to Impact's roster.

"You coming?" Derrick asked.

I got out of the car, and we headed to the auditorium, where we met Kyle, who was also graduating. Loretta was only a junior, so she was still in class, but knowing her, she would find a way to come to the auditorium to hang out with us.

"Did you hear about DC?" I asked Kyle as we waited for practice to start.

"Yeah. I'm not surprised he's been arrested. I told you he's bad news. Did you ever talk to him?"

I stood to let a few kids into our row; then I told him about the job.

He nodded. "That will be good exposure for you," he said. "It's coming at a good time, too. Let's make up some flyers announcing that you'll be in All-City so that you have a lot of support behind you. We can pass them out at Twilight every week."

"That's if I still have the gig," I said.

Kyle shrugged. "If not, we'll get you another one. It's not like you're not good at what you do."

Before I could respond, our senior class advisor, Mrs. Winston, called us to order and went through a rundown of the ceremony. I tuned her out. I couldn't understand why we needed to practice walking in and out of the auditorium. We had all done it hundreds of times. A couple of lyrics popped into my head, so I grabbed my backpack, got out the notebook I usually kept with me and jotted them down.

I was humming, and so engrossed in what I was doing that it took a few seconds for it to register that Kyle was nudging me.

"What?" I said, annoyed.

Mrs. Winston was staring at me. I stared back, not having a clue what was going on.

"Miss Richardson, would you care to join us?" she asked.

"Oh." I jumped out of my seat and headed to the front of the auditorium. Derrick had gone up to ask her a question earlier, so he was already standing at the podium.

"I hope that's a copy of your speech," Mrs. Winston said, pointing at my notebook. She had been bugging me about my speech for the last two weeks.

"Uh, no, it's in my other one," I said, snapping the notebook shut in case she asked to see what I was working on.

"I want a copy of that speech when we practice on Wednesday, Miss Richardson. No excuses."

"Okay," I said, and turned around and rolled my eyes. I didn't see what the big deal was about writing down a speech. I had learned that I rapped best when I freestyled, and I figured the same would be true with my speech. She probably wasn't even going to read what I handed in, anyway.

I stood onstage while Derrick went over his speech; then we ran through the rest of the program, which consisted of everybody walking across the stage pretending to get their diplomas. It seemed that that piece of paper was going to remain a dream for a few kids, because several of them got pulled out of line and were told they wouldn't be graduating.

If it hadn't been so pathetic, I would have laughed. Those kids should have known by now they weren't getting their diplomas. It really made them look stupid to have even shown up for rehearsal.

School was letting out just as practice ended, and although I wanted to hang out, Derrick and I decided to head home. Just in case my deal was still in place with DC, I didn't want to give Mama any more reason to be mad at me.

We dropped Loretta off at some open call at Green Acres Mall for a modeling gig. I was so ready for her to get out of the car. She spent the entire drive critiquing models in some magazine, telling us why she should have gotten the job instead.

When we walked into the house, I grabbed the

mail and flipped through it while Derrick went to check on Mama. Right after we had taken the SATs junior year, Derrick and I had started getting letters from colleges across the country. Even though we had both decided to attend Morgan State in Maryland, schools were still recruiting us, so I had gotten used to three or four letters a day arriving for me. At the bottom of the pile was a manila envelope with DC Records' return address. I tore it open, and inside was the contract Jessica had promised.

I showed it to Derrick, who had headed into the den to watch TV after popping some popcorn.

"How's Mama?" I asked.

"She was asleep, and I didn't want to wake her."

I nodded. "I guess they still want me," I said as he read the cover letter and then the contract.

"Maybe it came before DC was arrested," he said, putting down the contract and flipping through the channels with one hand and wolfing down a handful of popcorn with the other.

"That's true. I hadn't thought about that. I'd better call Jessica." I looked around for DC's card, but I couldn't remember what I had done with it.

"Check the letterhead," Derrick said without taking his eyes off the screen.

I stuck out my tongue at him.

"I saw that," he said, still not looking at me.

I mushed him in the head, then ran into the other room when he picked up a pillow and aimed it at me.

After locating the phone number on the letterhead, I went to my room and called. Jessica sounded even more stressed than she had the first time I'd talked to her.

"Hi, it's Jasmine Richardson," I said.

"Hey," Jessica said, sounding relieved. "Reporters have been ringing the phone off the hook. Hang on a second." She clicked to the other line and came back a few seconds later. "Ugggh…they're driving me crazy," she said. "So what's up?"

"Yeah, I heard about DC getting arrested. Is everything okay over there?" I really wanted to ask if I still had my job, but I didn't want to seem so cold and insensitive.

"Everything's fine. Unfortunately, this isn't the first time this has happened. When you're a successful black businessman, somebody is always looking for a way to bring you down. Even though DC's not here, it's still business as usual. His partner, Ron, is keeping things moving."

"I didn't realize he had a partner," I said.

"Hang on," she said, clicking over again. A few

seconds later she was back. "Not many people know, but you're family, so I can tell you," she said, laughing as she continued the conversation as though we hadn't been interrupted.

"So does that mean I still have a job?"

"Of course. Unless you hear from me, DC or Ron, nothing has changed. Like I said, it's business as usual. Did you get the contract?"

"Yep. I'll get it back to you tomorrow," I said, realizing that that meant I had to tell my parents that evening.

Jessica and I talked for a few more minutes, until she got another call she had to take; then we hung up.

Since I wanted to get on Mama's good side, I decided to go ahead and start dinner. I looked in the freezer, trying to find something I could make quick. I finally decided on some spaghetti. I put the ground beef in the microwave to defrost, then grabbed some jarred spaghetti sauce and a box of pasta and set them on the counter before I went to join Derrick in the den, where he was watching an episode of *Wild 'N Out*.

When the timer went off on the microwave, I headed back to the kitchen, and Derrick followed me.

"So is DC still in jail?" he asked as I cooked the meat.

"Yeah, but I still have my job. I told Jessica I'd send the contract back tomorrow."

He nodded, then got up to put on the pasta.

"Can you believe we're graduating on Thursday?" I asked, sitting at the table.

"Nope," he said. "This school year really just flew by. We'll be in college in the fall."

"Not if we get this record deal," I said.

When he didn't respond, I looked up to find him staring at me strangely. "What?" I said.

"We're still going to college if we get the deal," he said firmly.

I shrugged. "If you say so."

He looked like he wanted to say something else, but Daddy walked in.

"If it isn't my two favorite kids," he said.

"Hey, Daddy." I walked over and kissed him on the cheek.

He and Derrick nodded at each other before Daddy headed to the refrigerator, where he grabbed a beer before settling at the kitchen table.

"How was your day?" he asked.

Derrick looked at me, and I knew it was now or never. "Actually, it was really good," I said.

Daddy patted his knee, indicating I should sit on it. I laughed and shook my head. Sometimes he still thought I was six instead of sixteen. "I'm sorry," he said. "I do it out of habit."

I sat down at the table next to him. "I got a job offer," I said, really excited.

"Really? Doing what?" Daddy asked, then took a sip of his beer.

"Deejaying every week at Twilight." Daddy frowned. "They're going to have teen nights," I said quickly. "There won't be any drugs or alcohol."

"What are you talking about?" Mama asked, walking into the room.

I groaned to myself. I'd been hoping that I could tell Daddy everything and he could pass the information on to Mama.

"Jas got asked to deejay at a teen party every week. It's a really great opportunity," Derrick said.

I smiled my thanks at him for having my back.

"That's great, baby," Daddy said, leaning over to give me a kiss.

"How are you feeling, Mama?" I asked, trying to gauge her mood.

"My headache's much better," she said, walking over to stir the ground beef. "Thanks for starting dinner. So tell us about this club thing."

I sucked my teeth and looked at the floor so no one would see me roll my eyes. Mama had absolutely no tolerance for anything dealing with music, always calling it a "thing." Derrick kicked me under the table, and when I looked at him, he shook his head, which meant I needed to chill.

I repeated the details, and she seemed unimpressed, although Daddy was really excited.

"I use to play that club back in the day. Remember, baby?" Mama didn't have a chance to respond before Daddy turned back to me and Derrick. "A lot of rap pioneers got their starts at that club. A lot of the younger cats did, too. It was a great place to vibe and just hang out," he said, grinning. Luckily he didn't wait for us to respond. He turned to me. "This will be great exposure for you."

"I know," I said, thankful that I had sold Daddy on the idea.

"It would be great exposure," Mama said with her back to us, "if she needed exposure, but since she's going to college, she can put this music thing on hold."

She dumped the spaghetti sauce into the meat, then turned to look at us. "Besides, you all seem to have forgotten—Jasmine and Derrick are on punishment for the rest of the summer. And after you got fresh with me last night, you deserve it."

Alarmed, Derrick and I looked at each other. I glanced at Daddy with pleading eyes, knowing he was a sucker for them. He smiled at me and winked before heading over to the stove, where he wrapped his arms around Mama.

"Baby, maybe we overreacted last night," he said, kissing her on the neck.

I wanted to throw up—they were too old for that mess—but I knew Daddy was doing this partly for my benefit.

Mama turned around in his arms. "You ain't slick. You keep at it, and you'll be on punishment for the rest of the summer, too," she said, pointing a wooden spoon at him.

"What?" he asked innocently, kissing her on the lips.

"You know those kids were wrong last night," she said, throwing a glance at us.

"But they're really sorry. Right, kids?"

I nodded so hard my curly hair was bouncing all over my head. "It won't happen again," I said as it occurred to me how I could seal the deal.

I jumped up and hurried over to them, but before I could tell them, Mama looked at me strangely. "You say *you've* got a job. Derrick's not going to be doing this with you?"

I glanced at Derrick, but there was really nothing he could say. "No. They just wanted me to do it."

"You keep saying 'they.' Who offered you this job?"

My first reaction was to get defensive. Mama had never asked me who I was working for before, but then, Derrick had always been with me. I knew if I told her DC Records, she wouldn't let me take the job.

"The club hired me. One of the teachers at school recommended me," I said quickly.

Mama looked at me like she knew I was lying. "So why is there a letter from DC Records on the coffee table?"

"Oh, that was because of the talent show. They just sent a letter congratulating us on winning." I couldn't believe how easily the lies were flowing. I didn't look at Derrick, but I knew he wouldn't say anything.

I changed the subject. "I forgot to tell you the best part of all," I said.

"What?" Daddy asked. Despite everything, he was still excited.

"They're going to pay me a thousand dollars every week for the entire summer, so I'll have the money to pay for school myself." The thought hadn't crossed my mind until a few minutes earlier, but I was desperate to get Mama and Daddy to say yes. Although they hadn't said so, I knew it was going to be a struggle putting me and Derrick through school at the same time, not to mention the cost for Derrick to go to med school after that.

Mama grew suspicious when I mentioned the part about college.

"A thousand dollars a week? Who pays a sixteen-year-old that kind of money?" she asked. "Are you sure?"

I nodded and turned to my brother. "Right, Derrick?"

"Yep. She'll be able to pay for school and still have some spending money," he said. "Shoot, she might be able to pay for me to go, too." He was teasing, and we all laughed.

"Maybe I should call them," Mama said.

"No," I yelled, and she looked at me like I had lost my mind. "Mama, I can't have you calling. I'll look unprofessional." I turned to Daddy. "Please, let me do this myself."

I thought about showing them the contract to prove that I wasn't lying about the money, but then they would know my deal was really with DC Records. I realized I was going to have to handle things myself. I had planned to have my Uncle Henry look over the contract before I signed it, but I knew he would tell Mama and Daddy, so that was out. I was on my own on this one.

chapter 4

The day of our graduation was extremely gray and dreary, but I was so excited. Finally, I was about to move on with my life.

I had sent my signed contract to Jessica over at DC Records, along with my own contract, and she had immediately sent it back complete with DC's signature. He had been released due to lack of evidence the day before, and I was relieved.

I stood in front of my mirror, trying to get my hair to cooperate. The weather was humid, which made my hair frizzy, so I finally decided to pin it up before slipping on my white sundress. Although I liked the dress, I was extremely uncomfortable, since I usually wore jeans and T-shirts.

"You look beautiful," Daddy said, watching me from the doorway.

"Thank you," I said. I smiled at him in the mirror as I applied my lip gloss.

"What happened to my baby?" he said.

I laughed and went to give him a hug. "I'll always be your baby, Daddy."

"I know," he said, kissing me on my forehead. He looked around my room, and his eyes landed on my turntable.

"Remember the first time I showed you one of those?" he said, pointing to it.

"Yeah. I was five. You were cleaning out the garage, and we found the turntable and some records in a box," I said, smiling at the memory.

"Even back then you had talent. Never lose sight of that," he said. "No matter what path you find in life, don't give up on your dreams. I think that's my one regret, that I didn't follow my heart."

"Why didn't you go back to music after Derrick was born?" I asked.

"I thought about it, but your mother and I agreed that it was best that I find something more stable."

"But you could have done it on the side," I said.

He nodded as he took a seat on my bed. "Yeah, I could have, but then I wouldn't have been able to spend much time with my son, and that was important to me. I didn't want to just be the daddy he knew from a distance."

"But you had so much talent," I said. Every now and then Daddy would play tapes of him and Uncle Henry, and they were really good.

"And so do you. That's why I'm telling you to never give up on your dreams."

Derrick came and stood in the doorway. "You guys ready?" he asked.

Daddy stood and nodded. "I'm so proud of you both," he said, gathering us to him for a hug.

We headed to the living room, where Mama was waiting with her camera. She made us put on our caps and gowns, and then we took what felt like ten thousand pictures before we piled into Daddy's Toyota 4Runner and headed to the school. Derrick and I had to go line up so I didn't get to see the rest of our family—our grandparents; Uncle Henry and his family; and Mama's sister, Lela, and her family had all come.

Derrick was pacing, nervous about giving his speech.

"You okay?" I asked.

He glanced up from the paper he was clutching and nodded.

"You're going to be great," I said.

"Thanks," he said as he pulled at his tie.

"Relax." I placed a hand on his shoulder, hoping my calmness would rub off on him.

"Mr. and Miss Richardson," Mrs. Winston said, "how are you this evening?"

"Fine," Derrick and I said, turning to greet her.

"Miss Richardson, I need to speak with you."

I gave Derrick one more smile of encouragement before I followed Mrs. Winston to a corner of the cafeteria where all the graduates were gathered.

"I read that speech you gave me at practice Wednesday," she said, shaking her head and looking annoyed.

"What was wrong with it?" I asked. I really hadn't expected her to read the notes I had turned in.

"It wasn't a speech," she said.

"Oh, I must have misunderstood you. Sorry," I said, and smirked.

She put her finger in my face, and I took a step back. "Little girl, don't play with me. You better not get up there and embarrass me."

I laughed under my breath. "What are you going to do if I do?" I said. "It's not like you can send me to detention."

I knew she wanted to say something, but instead,

she walked off and announced it was time to line up. Derrick and I took our places next to each other at the front of the line, and the graduation march began.

As we entered the auditorium, I thought back on the night Derrick and I had won All-District. I felt so happy that I was leaving school behind and getting on with my dream. I searched the crowd for my family, but there were so many people I almost gave up—until I saw the sign one of my cousins had made. I pointed it out to Derrick, and we waved.

The graduation ceremony was so boring that I wished I could sneak out. When we got to the part in the program where Derrick and I were supposed to speak, Derrick started getting really nervous and began bouncing his leg.

"Yo, Derrick, look at getting onstage like you're about to do a rap," I whispered. He nodded and flashed a grateful smile.

"And now it's time to hear from our valedictorians," Mrs. Winston said from the stage.

Derrick slowly walked to the stage, and he made it through his speech without tripping up. Finally, it was my turn.

Mrs. Winston gave me a look of warning, but I ignored her as I took the podium.

"Good evening," I began. "Teachers, administration, family and friends and the Queens Academy's amazing class of 2007." I had to stop because the roar from the seniors was so loud no one could hear me. "I'm so happy to stand here and say we made it through. It's time for us all to take things to the next level. Everybody go for yours, and don't settle for anything less. Congratulations and good luck."

My classmates gave me a standing ovation as I returned to my seat. Derrick just shook his head.

The rest of the ceremony was pretty much a blur, with the exception of the moment when Derrick and I actually received our diplomas. Mama was standing at the bottom of the stage to take our picture, and Mrs. Winston posed with us, like I was her favorite student. I didn't say a word, because I knew I never had to see her again.

Afterward, we headed back to the house, where Mama had laid out a spread. There were oxtails, curried goat, rice and peas, fried chicken, macaroni and cheese and greens, all of which Derrick and I loved, along with an ice cream cake from Baskin-Robbins. I ate so much I thought I would be sick.

After Mama cut the cake, everybody took a seat in the living room.

"So what do you guys have planned for the summer?" Uncle Henry asked.

I smiled. "I have a job," I said proudly.

"Really?" Uncle Henry said with interest.

"Yeah, I'm going to be deejaying at Twilight on the weekends."

Uncle Henry looked at Daddy and raised an eyebrow. "Really?"

"Yeah," I said.

"What about you, Derrick?"

"I have a job at Flushing Hospital," he said, and Uncle Henry nodded his approval.

"An internship?" he asked.

"No, I'll be working in the mailroom, but at least I have my foot in the door."

Uncle Henry frowned. "Why didn't you get an internship?"

"I thought I was too young," Derrick said. "I didn't find out that I could apply until about a month ago, and by then it was too late."

"You need to be more proactive," Uncle Henry said, and turned his head like he was dismissing him. "You know, Shawn has an internship at the White House for the summer; then she'll be starting law school in the fall," he said, nodding at his daughter and smirking at Daddy.

"Oh, that's cool," I said politely, although I really didn't care.

"Daniel is going to London next week," he added, smiling at his nerdy-looking son, who was a sophomore at Cornell.

After that, I tuned him out. He was always bragging on his kids, and I was tired of hearing about it. When the room grew silent, I saw it as my chance.

"Can we leave now?" I asked Mama. Some of our friends were having parties, and Derrick and I had been asked to perform at quite a few of them, but we decided not to, since we wanted to celebrate just like everyone else.

Mama nodded. We said our goodbyes and headed out after Mama shoved some money into our hands. Kyle had rented a hotel room, and a bunch of kids were spending the night. We were supposed to be partying all night long to celebrate our graduation and our independence. I'd been surprised when Mama had taken us off punishment as a graduation present. It had finally hit her that we would be leaving for college soon, so she was starting to let us go. It felt so good to be treated like an adult.

The following Thursday, I spent the day chilling, since Derrick was at work and I had the house to myself. It would be my first night deejaying at Twilight, and I wasn't sure what to expect.

By noon, I was bored out of my mind, so I decided to call Loretta and Kyle to see what they were getting into. Loretta's voice mail picked up, but I hung up. Her message went on for like two minutes, because she listed every way humanly possible to contact her in case it was an agent or something calling. I texted her, and she responded that she was at a photo shoot and that we could hook up later.

I called Kyle.

"Hey," I said after he picked up. "What are you doing today?"

"Just chilling," Kyle yelled. I could barely hear him over the thundering beats in the background.

"You want to hang out?"

"Cool." He turned down the radio, but not by much. "Where are we going?"

"There's a record shop in Hempstead I've been meaning to check out. We could go there," I said.

"Okay," Kyle agreed. "You driving?"

"Yeah," I said, wondering why he even bothered to ask. Kyle drove entirely too fast for me, and if at all possible, I avoided riding with him. "I'll pick you up in twenty minutes."

We hung up, and I ran to my room to change out

of my sweatpants and baggy T-shirt. I threw on a pair of my favorite jeans and a T-shirt with a picture of a vinyl album on the front and the words, I'D RATHER BE SCRATCHING on the back, then ran a comb through my curls. I checked my backpack to make sure I had my notebook and then I was out.

Kyle was outside tossing a football with his little brother, Tony, who had on a Batman costume, when I pulled in. Tony ran over to me, cape flying, as I got out of the car. "Hey, Jas," he said, giving me a hug.

He was only six, and Kyle said he had a crush on me, which I thought was so cute.

"Hey, Tony," I said, returning the hug. "You hanging out with your big brother?"

Tony nodded as he smiled, exposing his missing front teeth. "Do you want to come see my room?" he asked. "Mommy bought me some Batman sheets."

"Okay," I agreed. He grabbed my hand and pulled me inside, and Kyle followed.

It didn't take that long to check out Tony's room. The floor was covered with action figures, so I had to watch where I stepped. As we were heading back to the kitchen, we passed Kyle's room.

"Oh, I forgot to show you the flyer," he said. We headed into his room, and I sat in his desk chair while he booted up his computer.

"Jas, do you want some Kool-Aid? I made it," Tony said proudly.

"Sure," I said as Kyle shook his head.

Tony ran out of the room.

"You shouldn't have said yes," Kyle said.

"Why not?" I asked.

"He put too much sugar in it."

I leaned back in the chair. "Oh, man."

Tony returned a few minutes later with a huge cup filled with red Kool-Aid that was sloshing over the side. "Here," he said, thrusting the cup at me, spilling the Kool-Aid on my chair.

"Thank you," I said. I pretended to take a gulp and accidentally swallowed some. It was horrible. "Uh, Tony, could you go get me a paper towel so I can wipe up this Kool-Aid?"

"Okay," he said, and ran off.

I looked at Kyle and silently pleaded for help. He shook his head, grabbed the cup, then headed off, I assumed to the bathroom. He returned a few seconds before Tony, and I pretended I was just finishing the Kool-Aid. "That was really good," I said, patting him on the head.

He handed me the paper towel, and his smile was so big I could almost see his tonsils. "Do you want some more?" he asked.

"Uh, maybe next time," I said. "Kyle and I are getting ready to go."

"Can I come?" He climbed onto my lap and slung an arm around my shoulder, and in that moment, I realized how much he resembled Kyle.

"Maybe next time, little man." His eyes got glassy, like he was about to cry. "What about if I bring you something back?"

Instantly the tears faded. "Okay," he said. "I'll make a surprise for you while you're gone."

"Deal." I stuck my hand out so he could give me five; then he ran off, yelling, "Mommy, Jas is going to buy me a surprise, and I'm going to make her something!"

Kyle showed me the flyer announcing that Derrick and I would be competing at All-City, and after I made a few suggestions, he saved the changes and printed out the new version to take with us so we could make copies.

As we were heading out the front door, Kyle's mother appeared in the doorway of her office. She was a writer, so she worked from home, which drove Kyle crazy because she was always there.

"Hey, Jas," she said. "I'm sorry I didn't speak to you earlier. I'm on deadline. Where are you two going?"

"Just to hang out for a while," Kyle said.

"Where?" his mother asked.

"Just to the record store, Ma, dang."

She looked at him, and he shut up real fast. "You guys be careful," she said. She walked over and tried to give Kyle a hug, but he stepped back.

"See ya, Mrs. Adams," I said, waving.

Kyle threw up his hand but didn't say anything.

"What was that about?" I asked once we got to the car.

"She's just getting on my nerves," he said. "I'll be glad when I move on campus."

Kyle had decided to attend New York University, which really surprised me. When we were in elementary school, he used to always talk about going to California to go to school, but once we got to high school, he stopped talking about it. Now that I thought about it, it was after his dad died of a massive heart attack our sophomore year that the dreams of California had stopped. I realized Kyle wanted to be closer to his mother than he was willing to admit. Mr. Adams had owned a chain of doughnut shops and left them all to his wife. Kyle had told me once that with all the money they still made, his mother never had to work again, and he and Tony could go to any college they wanted.

When we got to the record shop, it was pretty much empty, which didn't really surprise me. I headed over to the sale bin to see if there was anything good, and I almost lost my mind when I flipped through and found a copy of "Rapper's Delight." That song was way before my time, but I still loved it, and I was excited about adding it to my collection. I found a couple more albums, then headed over to Kyle, who was busy reading a DJ magazine.

"Hey, where'd you get that?" I asked, grabbing it out of his hand.

He snatched it back. "There's another copy over there," he said, nodding toward the register.

I had never seen the magazine before, and I flipped through, hoping I would learn some new technique or something, but all it contained was stuff I already knew. I put the copy back.

"You ready?" I asked.

Kyle nodded. He put back his magazine, then picked up a stack of CDs.

"You're buying all those?" I asked. He had at least twenty of them in his hands.

"Yeah," he said, shrugging.

"Why don't you just download them to your iPod?" I asked.

"I like having the real thing," he said. "I can't study the liner notes if I download a song."

Kyle really wanted to be a producer, and he really studied his craft. He was constantly sharing information with me that I otherwise wouldn't have known.

As I stood around waiting for the cashier to ring up Kyle's stuff, I remembered my promise to get something for Tony.

I spotted a candy rack near the register, and as I was looking at the selection, this fine guy came and stood near me.

"Hey, aren't you Jazzy J?" he asked.

"You know it," I said, deciding on a pack of M&Ms for Tony. I grabbed them and turned to head back to the register.

"Yo, I caught your performance at All-District. It was tight, ma."

"Thanks," I said.

"Yo, can I get your number? Maybe we can hang out sometime."

"No," Kyle said, scaring me. I hadn't even seen him walk up.

The guy looked from Kyle to me. "Oh, it's like that?" he said. "Sorry, man." He walked away without saying anything else to me.

"Why'd you do that?" I asked Kyle as I went to pay for Tony's candy.

"Man, don't be messing with them fools," he said.

"Oh, what, should I be messing with someone like you?" I said, and laughed. When Kyle didn't say anything, I looked at him. "Man, why are you trippin'?"

He just looked at me and shook his head.

By the time I'd dropped Kyle off and made it back to my house, it was almost six o'clock. I grabbed the picture Tony had painted for me and headed inside, where I found Mama and Derrick sitting in front of the television.

"Where've you been?" Mama asked, not bothering to look up.

"I just hung out with Kyle today," I said. "You still coming tonight, right, Derrick?"

He looked at me and nodded. "I guess."

"What do you mean you guess? You have to be there," I said. "You know I've never performed without you." The thought of him not having my back really had me spooked. Derrick was like my good luck charm.

He sighed. "Jas, just chill. I had a long day at work today, and I just want to relax a few minutes. I'll go with you."

I nodded as I took a deep breath. Suddenly I felt nervous, which was never the case before I performed. I hurried to my room and pulled out the outfit I had selected. It was a red shirt that I was going to tie in a knot once I left the house so my belly button would be exposed, a pair of fitted jeans and some Air Force Ones. I thought about rocking some really nice high-heeled shoes, but I had learned my lesson one night a couple of years ago. By the end of that night, my feet had been hurting so bad I didn't think I would be able to walk for a week.

I made sure all my equipment was together and added my new albums to my crate of collectibles, which never left my room. The other crates I would have Derrick load in my car.

"I'm ready," I said a few minutes later.

Derrick hadn't moved from his spot on the sofa. I walked over to him, and he was sound asleep. I shoved him to wake him up. "Derrick," I whined, "you're not even dressed."

He just lay there for a minute like he was trying to figure out where he was. "Hurry up," I said, glancing at the clock on the cable box. "I'm going to be late." It was already six-thirty.

Derrick took a deep breath and tried to stand up.

Finally he flopped back down. "Why don't you go by yourself?" he said. "I'm tired from running around and delivering mail all day."

My mouth dropped open as I looked at him. "You can't be serious," I said.

"Jas, you'll be fine. Loretta and Kyle will be there."

"Yeah, but they're not you. I've never performed without you," I said. "I don't want to jinx myself. You have to come. You have to." I grabbed his arm and pulled him up.

He looked like he wanted to say something, but he changed his mind.

"Derrick," I said, "we're gonna be late."

He walked out of the room without looking at me and returned a few seconds later with one of the crates.

"Aren't you going to change clothes?" I asked. He had on a pair of khaki pants and a white button-down, both of which were wrinkled.

He shook his head. "I wouldn't want you to be late," he said sarcastically.

I rolled my eyes at him. "Look, I'm sorry if I'm acting funky, but I'm just a little nervous."

Derrick's attitude melted almost as quickly as it had begun. In a lot of ways, he reminded me of Daddy. They both had a soft spot for me, and I knew it.

We loaded the car and took the short drive to Twilight. The place was nothing like I had expected. It was actually my first time ever being in a club, and I guess I had imagined that they were all ritzy and upscale—at least, that was the way they looked on TV.

This one smelled like stale sweat and cigarette smoke, and it was so dark I wondered how people would see each other. The furniture looked like it hadn't been replaced in years, and there was a huge crack in the mirror behind the bar, which was not a good sign. It just made sense to me that the only way that crack could have gotten there was if someone had thrown something—or someone.

"You okay?" Derrick asked, sensing my nervousness.

"Yeah, I'm cool," I said. I took a deep breath and looked around before rubbing my hands together. "Let's get set up."

Derrick and I quickly unloaded my equipment; then I went to find the manager, who had let us in.

"Is there anything else I need to do?" I asked. The club wasn't supposed to open for another twenty minutes, and I figured people wouldn't start showing up until an hour after that, since no one wanted to be the first to arrive.

"Nah, you can just chill," he said. He was a big, burly guy who looked like he used to be in shape a long time ago. "You want a drink?"

I hesitated. Other than a sip of champagne I had had at my cousin Janelle's wedding earlier that year, I had never had anything to drink, but the thought was tempting.

"She's fine," Derrick said. I hadn't even heard him walk up. "You know she's only sixteen, right?"

The manager shrugged.

"Is it okay if we go outside for a few minutes?" I asked, thinking that the fresh air would help to pass the time.

"Sure," he said, "but I can't be responsible for your equipment."

Derrick and I looked at each other, and I wondered what I'd gotten myself into.

"That's okay," I said. "We'll just wait over there." I pointed to my equipment.

The guy shrugged again. "Suit yourself," he said.

Derrick and I walked over to my turntable in silence. Once we thought the guy couldn't hear us anymore, he asked, "Are you sure you want to do this? I'm not getting a good vibe about this place, Jas."

"Quit tripping," I said. "Everything is gonna be fine." I hoped I was telling the truth.

* * *

I was surprised when a few people trickled in a little after eight. By then the manager, whose name was Lenny, had turned on some track lights, which did wonders for the place. Once I put on some music, I felt at home, and I was ready for whatever the night held.

There were at least a hundred kids in the place within the first hour. I looked around for Derrick, and he was sitting at the bar checking things out. Loretta and Kyle had also arrived, and they were both on the dance floor having a good time. I couldn't help but smile as I nodded to the beat.

I finally decided to take a break around ten, when I had to pee so bad I thought my bladder would burst. I got Derrick's attention, and he came over to relieve me for a few minutes.

On the way back from the bathroom, I stopped at the bar to get a soda and gulped it down before I headed back to the DJ booth. Lenny, who was also working the bar, handed me another drink, and I smiled my thanks before snaking my way through the people on the crowded dance floor.

"Hey, girl," Loretta sang when she spotted me. She threw her arms around me and gave me a hug. "This party is on point. You've been playing all my jams."

"Thanks," I yelled over the music. "I've got to get back to work."

She nodded and turned back to her dance partner, some light-skinned dude who reminded me of Usher.

Derrick had pulled out a stack of albums for me, and I thanked him. "You thirsty?" I asked.

He nodded and took my cup from me. "I forgot how hot it gets behind this table," he said, taking a gulp. He frowned as he swallowed it. "What is this?" he asked, holding the cup up and peering at the bottom.

"Sprite," I said.

He took another tiny sip. "This is not Sprite. Where'd you get it?"

"Lenny gave it to me."

Derrick glared over at the bar. "I'll be back," he said.

"Where are you going?" I yelled just as the music went off. With the sudden silence, everyone heard me, and it seemed as though every eye in the room was on my brother as he walked over to the bar.

I grabbed an album and put it on, hoping to draw everyone's attention back to the music, but like me, most of them were still watching the scene at the bar. Although I couldn't hear what Derrick was saying, it was pretty obvious that he was upset.

He pointed at the cup, then pointed at me, and

before I knew it, Lenny had punched him twice in the face. By the time it finally occurred to me what had happened, Derrick was on the floor with a crowd standing over him. I ran to him and started screaming when I saw all the blood.

"Are you crazy?" I yelled at Lenny. He looked like he was about to punch me, too, but I didn't care. "How could you hit my brother?"

Lenny went back to serving drinks like nothing had happened, and I finally figured out why Derrick was upset. "Did you spike my drink?" I asked.

Lenny went back to drying glasses, but I saw a small smile creep across his face.

"What's wrong with you?" I screamed. "This is supposed to be an alcohol- and drug-free environment. Why would you do something like that, you jerk?"

Before Lenny could answer, Kyle was at my side, and together we helped up Derrick while Loretta applied a napkin to his nose.

"Man, let's get out of here. This guy is crazy," Kyle said with disgust.

"You know we're pressing charges," Loretta screamed, placing her hand on her hip and rolling her neck so her waist-length weave flowed from side to side.

"Get back to work," Lenny ordered, but I just looked at him and rolled my eyes. "I said get back to work—now."

I kept walking like I hadn't heard him. It wasn't until we were halfway to the car that I realized my equipment was still inside the club.

"Oh, man," I said.

"What's wrong?" Loretta asked. She was still holding the napkin to Derrick's nose, but it was soaked with blood.

"I left my equipment back there."

"Don't worry about it," Kyle said. "We'll come back and get it tomorrow."

Derrick and I looked at each other, and I shook my head. "No, we've got to go get it now. I don't think it'll be here tomorrow if we wait."

Derrick removed Loretta's hand from his nose. It was a little swollen, but other than the blood he seemed okay. "Come on," he said, and turned back toward the club.

I thought about arguing, but I decided not to. When my brother made up his mind to do something, there was no stopping him.

We headed back to the club, and I walked in to find some big hairy dude using my equipment. Derrick didn't stop walking until he was standing in front of the guy. Without a word, he picked up a crate of albums and handed it to Kyle. He handed another one to Loretta, then he began unplugging my equipment.

The crowd groaned in unison, and people started turning to see what was going on.

The big hairy dude looked like he was ready to fight. I pulled out my cell phone and called 911 just as Lenny reached us.

"What do you think you're doing?" he asked.

Derrick continued neatly wrapping my electrical cords without saying a word.

Lenny got in his face, and I looked around for a weapon to defend my brother.

Derrick handed me some of the smaller pieces of my equipment just as Kyle and Loretta were walking through the door. Kyle came over and they picked up the heavier pieces and we headed out the door. Before we could make it, Lenny blocked the exit.

"The party's not over yet," he said, silently daring us to leave.

"Yes, it is," Derrick said quietly, and tried to make his way around Lenny, but the manager was so huge he was totally blocking the entrance.

I prayed the cops would arrive soon, and I was happy when I heard the siren in the distance. I looked around the crowd, and most of the kids there were staring at us, so I didn't have a lot of hope that they would help us, since no one had jumped in the first time Lenny had hit Derrick.

Derrick and Lenny stood glaring at each other, and when I heard an authoritative voice boom "What's going on here?" relief filled me—until I looked at the imposing figure standing in the doorway.

chapter 5

DC was even bigger than Lenny, and he did not look happy, especially when he realized the cops were on their way.

Lenny stepped aside to allow DC to enter, and DC towered over me. He was dressed in a white suit with a red shirt and a white tie, and his red wide-brimmed hat hid his eyes. "You okay?" he asked, looking really concerned.

I nodded. "He spiked my drink and hurt my brother," I said, pointing at Lenny. I felt like I was four years old for telling, but I knew DC was the one who could make things right.

DC looked at the club, then turned to Lenny, and he was so angry that veins were bulging in his thick neck. "Have you lost your mind?" he bellowed, and I took a step back, as if his words could slap me.

Lenny shrugged. "What's the big deal? The kid needed to loosen up."

"Clear the club," DC growled to his men. Within seconds the kids were hanging out on the sidewalk.

DC towered over Lenny, murder in his eyes. "I told you I wanted to run a clean operation this time. I'm in enough trouble as it is. You better hope I don't get arrested again."

Lenny still didn't look concerned. "Man, chill. The kid is fine."

DC didn't say a word, I assumed because he spotted the cops. He nodded at one of the men with him, and the guy went outside and talked to the cops, who left a few minutes later. After that, DC signaled another man who grabbed Lenny by the arm and led him toward the back of the club. DC seemed to finally realize Derrick and I were staring at him. He turned to us and smiled, which instantly transformed his face.

"I didn't mean to give you guys a show," he joked, "but that clown got me upset."

We laughed weakly, but I think we were both trying to figure out whether we should be scared. Derrick had his hand on my arm and wouldn't let go.

"Party's over tonight, kids," DC announced from

the door of the club, and a few people on the sidewalk groaned. "Don't worry. We'll be back next week in a different location. To make up for any inconvenience, why don't you guys head on over to McDonald's and order whatever you want, my treat. I'll also make sure you guys get into next week's party for free."

After that, the kids were fine. DC nodded at another member of his crew. The guy left the building and returned a few minutes later with a brown box. He pulled out CDs and a permanent marker and began writing something on them before handing them to everyone on the sidewalk. As the kids started to leave, another member of DC's team handed everyone twenty dollars so they could go to McDonald's.

"You sure you're okay?" DC asked, turning to Derrick and me.

I nodded.

"Listen, I'm going to find another location for the parties—somewhere you guys will feel safe and can have a good time without having to worry. Will you come back and deejay next week?"

Derrick was squeezing my hand, which was my signal to say no. I glanced at him out of the corner of my eye, but his expression didn't change, although he did squeeze my hand a little harder.

"Uh…" I began.

I guess DC could sense that I was about to say no. He pointed to a table. "Let's talk," he commanded. DC nodded at a guy he introduced as his partner, Ron, and they headed to a table.

I didn't feel as though I had any choice but to sit down. Derrick sat right next to me.

"What can I do to make you come back?" he asked.

"Nothing," Derrick said, speaking for me.

DC ignored him. "Jasmine, I think you're very talented, and I would love to work with you. I'm sure you probably know that I don't have the greatest image in the world, but I'm trying to change all that. I'm trying to bring some fresh new talent to my label and get away from gangsta rap. I think you're exactly what I'm looking for. If you come back and deejay the club, I guarantee you I'll give you a record deal."

My mouth dropped open in amazement. My dream was finally coming true.

Before I could say yes, Derrick jumped in. "She doesn't need your record deal. We're going to win All-City and get a deal with Image."

DC chuckled as he stuck a cigar in his mouth.

"Then you'll just be settling for second best. I'm

the reason Image is what it is today. Kevin Mitchell was my protégé. Right, Ron?"

Ron simply nodded. The fact that he hadn't taken his eyes off Derrick the entire time we had been sitting at the table was kind of weird, but I tried not to let it get to me.

"She's not playing any more of your events," Derrick said. I had never seen him so determined, and truthfully, it annoyed me. He was messing up my shot at my dream, and I wasn't having it.

Before I could voice my thoughts, DC turned to me. "I promise you we'll find a new location, and I'll pay you an extra five hundred dollars a week." He reached into his pocket and pulled out a huge wad of cash. He peeled off a few hundreds and handed them to me. "Here's two thousand for this week because of all the trouble. I promise it won't happen again."

My eyes grew big. I was going to make fifteen hundred dollars every week for a few hours' work, and I was leaving there with two grand?

"Okay," I said before DC could change his mind.

"Jasmine, what are you doing?" Derrick asked, looking at me like I was crazy.

DC turned to Derrick and peeled off some more money and held it out to him. "Here you are, for your troubles. I apologize for Lenny. I assure you he'll be dealt with."

Derrick pretended he hadn't heard DC as he turned to me. "Jasmine, what are you doing?" he repeated.

I ignored him as I looked at DC and gave him my best smile. "I'll call you next week to find out where the event is going to be held."

DC nodded. "I'll be out of town for a while. You can just deal with Ron."

"Okay," I agreed.

Once we made it outside, I turned to my brother, not able to hold in my anger any longer.

"Have you lost your mind?" I yelled. "You almost messed up this gig for me."

"What happened?" Loretta asked. She and Kyle had waited outside while we talked to DC.

I briefly filled her in, and she looked at Derrick like he was crazy.

"How you gon' tell your sister to turn down this opportunity?" she said. "This is the chance of a lifetime." She looked at me. "If I were you, I'd take it."

"Don't worry. I am," I said, looking at my brother in disgust.

"Your brother was just looking out for you," Kyle

said softly once I was done. "I would have done the same thing."

"Man, both of y'all are crazy if you think I'm turning down fifteen hundred dollars a week. I'll still have enough to pay for school, plus I'll have plenty of spending money left over. Best of all, DC has guaranteed me a record deal. All my dreams are coming true," I said as we headed to the car.

"Yeah, but at what cost?" Derrick asked.

I ignored him.

We said our goodbyes to our friends, then headed home. During the drive, I thought about how Derrick had had my back and had even been willing to fight for me.

"Look, I'm sorry about the way I treated you. I know you were just looking out for me," I said. "Please don't tell Mama and Daddy what happened."

"Whatever, Jas," he said, staring out the window.

"Derrick, this is my big chance. You know if you tell Mama and Daddy they won't let me go back."

He turned to look at me, and even in the darkness I could see traces of blood on his nose and make out that one eye was shiny and starting to turn purple. I refocused on the road, but I knew he had seen me looking at his eye.

"How would you like me to explain this?" he asked, pointing at his eye.

I didn't respond since I didn't know how we could explain that. "I'll think of something," I said lamely, and he just shook his head.

Surprisingly my parents hadn't made it home by the time we pulled into the driveway. Every now and then they went out, but neither of them had mentioned anything about any plans before we left.

Derrick and I entered the house in silence, and he went to his room and I went to mine. I flipped on my television, more for background noise than anything, and started getting ready for bed.

After my shower, I put on my pajamas, then headed into the kitchen for a snack. Derrick was in the kitchen, too, and he totally ignored me, which I wasn't used to.

"You want some cookies?" I asked, trying to make peace with him.

He shook his head.

"I'm going to microwave some chocolate chip cookies. You know they're your favorite, especially when they're hot." I pulled out the cookies and placed them on a plate, then stuck them in the microwave.

As they warmed, I watched Derrick eat a

sandwich. When I noticed his cup was almost empty, I jumped up and got him another soda. "Please don't be mad at me," I said as I placed the can next to his plate.

Derrick sighed and looked at me. "DC is trouble. I can feel it. I think you're in over your head, Jas. Think about it, why is it so important that he sign you?"

"Because I'm good. There is no other female out there like me," I said. I got up to grab the cookies when the microwave timer went off.

"Yeah, we both know you're good, but he seems to be going out of his way to get you. Why? I don't trust him. You're going to get a record deal," he said. "As soon as you win All-City, you can sign with Image, which has a much better reputation. Leave DC alone."

"What about the money for school?" I said. "You know Mama and Daddy could really use that money if I decide to go to college."

Derrick sighed. "Yeah, that's true, but they can find a way to pay. Or we can always take out student loans," he said.

I placed the plate of cookies between us before going to pour myself a glass of milk. When I returned to the table, Derrick was still sitting there deep in thought.

"Okay, what if you play the clubs, but when he offers you a deal, you say no?" he proposed.

I didn't like the idea, but I was willing to agree to anything just so my brother wouldn't be mad at me. "Okay," I agreed. "Thanks, Derrick."

The next morning, I woke up and realized I had fallen asleep with the television on. My mother hated when I did that, and I was surprised she hadn't come in and turned it off in the middle of the night.

I was flipping through channels, trying to find out what the weather was going to be, when a news broadcast caught my eye. There on the screen was a picture of Lenny, the manager of Twilight. In the photo he looked much younger, and he was definitely much thinner, but I still recognized him. I turned up the volume with the remote.

"Details are still sketchy," the anchor was saying, "but it looks as though Leonard Miller fell asleep at the wheel and his car crashed into a telephone pole in the wee hours of the morning. The car burst into flames, and a passerby was unable to free Miller."

I sat on my bed as I stared at the screen with my mouth wide open. I blocked out the rest of what was being said as the image of one of DC's men leading

Lenny to the back of the club flooded my mind. Something told me Lenny's death wasn't an accident.

I decided that if no one said anything to me about Lenny's death, I wasn't going to mention it. He shouldn't have spiked my drink. Karma got him.

Luck was on my side, because by the time I made it downstairs after showering and getting dressed, Daddy and Derrick were already gone. The house was quiet, so I thought Mama was gone, too, until she appeared in the kitchen a few minutes later.

"Good morning," she said cheerfully.

"Good morning," I said, trying to force some cheer into my voice.

Mama walked over to the refrigerator and grabbed a carton of orange-strawberry-banana juice. She poured herself a glass, then held the container up for me, silently asking if I wanted some. I shook my head. My mind was still on Lenny's death, and I really didn't think I could keep anything down.

"Do you have anything you want to tell me?" she asked.

"What do you mean?" I asked nervously.

"Derrick told me and your daddy what happened last night," she said, looking at me. I couldn't read her expression. I got up from the table and grabbed a box of cereal from the cabinet just to give me something to do.

"What did he say?" I asked. My brother had promised he wouldn't tell Mama and Daddy what went down, but maybe he had seen the news about Lenny and changed his mind.

"That he had to beat up some guy for hitting on you."

I breathed a sigh of relief. "It was no big deal," I said, shrugging. I didn't want to say too much, because I didn't want to contradict Derrick's story.

"I think the fact that your brother is sporting a black eye and a busted lip is a big deal," she said. She stilled my hand from pouring the cereal and forced me to look at her.

"Jas baby, you can't let anybody disrespect you, okay?"

"Okay, Ma," I said before focusing on my cereal.

She cupped my chin, forcing me to gaze into her eyes. I don't know what she saw in mine, but she led me to a chair at the kitchen table.

"You okay?" she asked softly.

My tears betrayed me as I nodded.

Mama grabbed me and hugged me, running her hand up and down my back like she did when I was a little girl. "Oh, sweetie. It's okay. That guy won't hurt you. I promise you that."

I pulled back and looked at her, wondering how she knew about what had happened with DC, but then I realized she was talking about the guy who was supposed to have hit on me.

I wiped my tears with my hands and nodded.

"So, what do you have planned today?" I asked to change the subject.

"I'm going to get my hair and nails done, but after that I'm free. Maybe we can hang out this afternoon—have a girls-only day," she suggested.

"You mean night," I joked. Going to get her hair and nails done on a Saturday could take all day.

She laughed before she got up and grabbed my bowl and finished pouring my cereal for me. "You can reach me on the cell if you need me," she said. "Daddy and Derrick went to get some part for Derrick's car, and I think they had a few more errands to run, so they might not be back until later. Looks like you have the house to yourself."

"I think I'll call Loretta," I said. "Maybe we can hang out until you get back."

"That sounds like fun," Mama said. She kissed me on the forehead and then she was gone.

After I finished eating, I got dressed; then I called

Loretta. Normally I liked having the house to myself—it gave me a chance to play my music loud as I worked on beats and songs without anyone complaining—but the thought of being alone after what I'd seen on the news frightened me.

Loretta answered on the first ring. "Hey, girl," she said.

"Hey," I responded. "What are you getting into today?"

"I'm trying to decide what to wear to this job interview I have later today."

"Can I come over?"

"Sure," she said. "You can give me your opinion."

Later that day, I still couldn't shake Lenny's image out of my mind, although hanging out with Loretta was a welcome distraction.

I was lying across her bed in her tiny bedroom, trying to relax as she stood in the mirror flipping through a magazine, trying to copy the models' poses.

"Did you hear about that guy from the club?" she asked suddenly.

I thought I would pass out from shock, but I managed to play it off.

"Yeah," I said as casually as I could, although my

voice cracked. "Isn't that crazy? I mean, we just saw him last night." I took a peek at her to see if she noticed anything, but she was still focusing on her poses. "Do you think DC had anything to do with it?" I asked. The question had been running through my mind all day, and I was relieved to finally be able to talk about it with someone.

Loretta smoothed her purple satin minidress before she turned and looked at me. "Of course not," she said. "Why would he have that man killed?"

"I don't know..." I said, wondering if my imagination was just working overtime.

Loretta turned back to the mirror. "What do you think I should wear to my interview?"

"Is it for another gig?" I asked, glad she had changed the subject. I got up off the bed and walked over to her closet. Although it was small, clothes were spilling out of it, and out of her drawers, as well.

It took us about an hour to come up with what Loretta decided was the perfect outfit: black pants, a white blouse and a printed scarf, which she decided to wear as a belt.

We headed out to Popeye's for lunch, and on the drive it occurred to me that Loretta was interviewing for an actual job rather than a modeling gig.

"What's up with the job?" I asked during a break in music.

"I need to get some new pictures taken for my book," she said, referring to her modeling portfolio.

"But didn't you do that a couple of months ago?" I asked.

She grabbed a piece of gum out of her purse before offering me one, which I took. "Yeah, but I haven't been getting good feedback on them, so I decided I need to take some more. Word is one of DC Records' artists is going to be casting for his video soon, and I want to get the job."

I nodded thoughtfully. "Most of those guys have women on their covers with their butts hanging all out."

Loretta shrugged. "It's not a big deal. You do what you have to do for what you're passionate about, right? Besides, why waste this incredible body I have?"

I took my eyes off the road to look at her in amazement. "You would actually be willing to take off your clothes to land a job?" I asked incredulously.

"Yeah. What's the big deal?" she asked. "I think posing for *Playboy* would be kind of cool."

"Girl, you're only sixteen. Your mom would kill you for posing half-naked."

Loretta shook her head. "So? This is my life, and I'm going to live it. Before I leave this earth, people will know my name."

When I made it home from hanging with Loretta, Mama still wasn't back, which didn't really surprise me.

I didn't see Daddy's car in the driveway, either, so I figured he and Derrick were still out. I decided I would practice for All-City since I still had the place to myself.

I stuck my key in the door, already focusing on my music. When the door was opened from the inside, it scared me so bad I lost my breath.

"Scared ya, huh?" Derrick asked.

I popped him on the arm as I walked past. "Boy, you are so silly. You scared the fool out of me." He followed me into the kitchen, where I grabbed a soda from the fridge. "What are you doing here?" I asked.

"Daddy decided to surprise Mama with a night out, so the minute she walked in the door he made her turn around so they could leave. Good thing she had on a nice outfit, 'cause Daddy wasn't trying to hear letting her go change."

He laughed and shook his head.

"We were supposed to hang out tonight," I said, disappointed. Although Mama and I had our share of problems, I really did enjoy spending time with her.

"You want to hang out with me instead?" Derrick asked. "We can go to the movies."

"That's okay," I said. "There's nothing I wanna see. Why don't we get something to eat, then practice for All-City? We can be as loud as we want since Mama and Daddy aren't here."

"Okay," Derrick agreed.

We decided to order pizza, and by the time it arrived we had already been working for almost an hour. I peeled a hundred off the wad DC had given me the night before and waited while the delivery guy gave me change.

Derrick and I settled down to eat. As he chewed thoughtfully on his third slice of ham and pineapple pizza, he looked at me.

"What?" I said, reaching for a napkin to wipe the cheesy goo off my face.

"You really gon' go back and work for DC?"

I frowned at him. "Yeah," I said. "What part of 'fifteen hundred dollars' didn't you understand?"

Derrick just shook his head.

"What?" I asked, really getting annoyed.

"I can't believe you."

I rolled my eyes. "Like you wouldn't take the money if it was offered to you. You're just jealous that you weren't given the chance to make it."

As soon as the words came out of my mouth, I regretted saying them. "I'm sorry," I said quickly.

Derrick just looked at me and gave this dry laugh. "You really think I'm jealous of you?" he asked.

I didn't respond, although I was thinking, *Who wouldn't be jealous?*

"Girl, you're going to learn that money isn't everything. You've heard the horror stories about DC just like I have. Don't sell your soul just to make a quick dollar," he said, sounding like Daddy.

"Whatever," I said. I headed to my room and decided to call Loretta.

"How was your job interview?" I asked.

"I got it!" she said, and I hadn't heard her sound so excited in a long time.

"Congratulations," I said. "You never did tell me what the position is for."

"Oh, that's the great part," she said. "I'm going to be working for *Hot*."

"You mean that magazine with the half-naked women on the cover?"

"Yeah," she said excitedly. "I'm going to be a photo assistant, so I'll get to go to the shoots and everything. This should be great for my modeling career."

I wondered about Loretta's sudden fascination with being half-naked, but before I could say anything else, she started talking again.

"I found out Madd Dogg is casting for his video next week. Do you think you could loan me five hundred dollars so that I can get my new pictures done? I promise I'll pay you back."

"Sure," I said without hesitation. What good was earning extra money if I couldn't help my friends?

"Cool. I'll come get it tomorrow."

"Okay," I agreed. "Well, I guess I'll chill for a little while before bed. See you tomorrow."

"Bye," she said, and we hung up.

DC's assistant, Jessica, called me first thing Monday morning. I didn't even hear the phone ring. It wasn't until Derrick came and tossed the cordless onto my chest that I jumped up, trying to figure out what was going on.

"Jasmine, I just wanted to give you the information for the new venue," Jessica said.

"Okay," I said, knowing I sounded like I was still

asleep. I cleared my throat as I grabbed my note-book and a pen from my nightstand. "I'm ready."

"It's Club Horizon on Merrick Boulevard in Lau-relton."

"Oh, yeah, I know where that is. It's not too far from my mom's job. It just opened, right?"

"Yes," Jessica said. "I think you're really going to like the place."

"I hope so," I said.

By the time Thursday rolled around, Derrick was speaking to me again, and I was glad. I hated when we argued.

"You're still coming tonight, right?" I asked.

"I can't," he said.

I waited for him to elaborate, but he didn't. "Why not?" I finally asked. "You're not still mad, are you?"

He shook his head. "No, I'm not mad at you, but I don't agree with what you're doing. Ask Kyle to go with you."

"Derrick," I whined, "you always go. Please come."

He shook his head, and there was something in his eyes that let me know that he wasn't going to change his mind.

"Fine," I said. I turned around to storm out of the den.

Just as I reached the threshold, he called out to me. "Jas."

I tried to hide my smile, figuring he had changed his mind. "Yes?" I said.

"I'm also thinking about not performing in All-City."

"What?" I screamed. I ran back over to him. "Derrick, quit tripping. What do you mean you're thinking about not performing? We're about to land a record deal. Our dream is about to come true."

"No, your dream is about to come true," he said. "You know performing isn't what I want to do. We're starting college in a couple of months. I don't want to record an album."

I looked at him in amazement. What he was saying really wasn't a surprise. "Are you doing this because you're still mad at me about the other night? I apologize. I know you're not jealous of me," I said.

He laughed. "You know, everything doesn't revolve around you, Jasmine," he said.

I looked at him. "What's this really about?" I asked.

He just shook his head. "I told you," he said.

"I've been busy living your dreams. I'm not going to do that anymore. It's time I live my own life."

I made it to the club, but I was still angry at my brother, and it showed in my performance. I pretty much just let the records play without putting the spin on the songs for which I was becoming known. Everyone seemed to be having a good time, but I knew I wasn't on point.

Kyle was on the dance floor with some girl I'd never seen before, but every now and then I would catch him looking at me. I tried to smile to reassure him that I was okay, but I knew the smile never reached my eyes. On the drive over I had briefly told him about what had happened with Derrick, and he hadn't seemed surprised.

Loretta had come along, too. She had a long ponytail weave and she was backing that thang up so hard on the dance floor that she kept slapping her partner in the face with it. If I hadn't been in such a foul mood, it would have been funny.

I put on another song and was thinking about taking a break when someone put a cup down next to me. I figured it was Kyle, who was always looking out for me, but when I looked up to say thanks, my mouth fell open.

"Do you know who you are?" I asked the tall, brown-skinned guy.

Triple T's name was everywhere lately. He had produced a string of hits for a lot of artists, including several for DC Records. I had seen an interview with him the night before, and I was really impressed. He wasn't that much older than me—I think he said he was nineteen—yet he was passionate about music just like me.

He gave this deep, sexy laugh. "Yeah, I know who I am. The question is who are you?" he said.

"My name is Jasmine Richardson, but my fans call me Jazzy J," I said.

"Nice to meet you, Jasmine Richardson." He shook my hand and pushed the drink toward me. "I thought you might be thirsty," he said.

"Thank you," I said, suddenly realizing how hot it was in the club—or had Triple T's presence just done that to me? I was just about to take a sip when I remembered what had happened the last time I was in a club. He didn't look like the type to spike someone's drink, but then I didn't really know him.

"Aren't you going to drink it?" he asked, and smiled. I realized he didn't have his gold grill in, and he looked much better without it. His teeth were white and even, which I loved. I was a sucker for brown-skinned men with pretty teeth.

"Nah, I'm cool," I said.

"Smart girl," he said, nodding in approval.

"Did you put something in my drink?" I asked, relieved that I had followed my gut.

"Nah," he said, shaking his head. He had on a baseball cap that was covering his eyes, but I knew they were hazel because they had shown a close-up shot of him in the interview I'd seen. "But you're right. You don't know me, and I respect that you decided not to drink what's in that cup."

"What's in it?" I asked.

He grinned, and I noticed he had an adorable dimple in his left cheek. "Water."

I laughed and decided to trust him. I took a sip, and as he had promised, there was just water in the cup. "Thanks," I said before I turned my attention to the music. I put on a few more songs and tried not to let it show that I was excited that he was waiting so patiently for me to finish.

"I've been hearing a lot of good things about you," he said when I was done.

Before I could respond, Loretta came over and threw herself into his arms. "Triple T, I thought that was you," she said. She gave him a big kiss on the cheek.

I frowned. "I didn't know you guys knew each other," I said.

Loretta laughed. "We don't," she said. "I've just seen him so much on television and in magazines that I feel like he's fam."

Although I was glad Loretta didn't know him, I didn't appreciate the way she had thrown herself at T.

He looked a little embarrassed and tried to extricate himself from the death grip Loretta had on his arm.

"Girl, go sit down somewhere," I said.

Loretta swayed a little, and I realized she was drunk. I wondered where she'd gotten the liquor, since everything in the club was on the up-and-up— there was no sign of alcohol or drugs—but I figured I'd find out about that later.

"Why you trippin'?" she asked, slurring her words.

"No, why are you trippin'?" I asked. "You see we're trying to have a conversation."

"Whatever," she said. She reached into her purse and pulled out a modeling comp card that featured her in different poses and had her phone number on it, then handed it to Triple T. "If you or someone you know is ever looking for a model, look no further," she said. She winked at him, trying to look sexy, then squeezed his bicep before walking away.

"I'm sorry," I said. "That girl is crazy, but you gotta love her."

Triple T just laughed.

"So what are you doing here?" I asked.

"I came to see you," he said, smiling.

"Me?" I asked.

"Yeah. I heard there was this hot DJ doing Teen Scene in Queens, so I decided to come check you out. Nobody told me how cute you are, though."

I blushed and glanced down at the floor. When I looked up, Kyle had stopped dancing and was staring right at me. He looked like he was about to come over, but I shook my head.

"You're really good. You seem like you've got a lot on your mind tonight, though," Triple T said, drawing my attention from Kyle.

"You can tell that from my music?" I asked.

He nodded.

"Wow, you're really good. I do have some things on my mind."

"You want to talk about it? I'm a good listener."

"That's really nice of you," I said. "Maybe I'll take you up on that offer."

"Maybe you should," he said. "What are you doing tomorrow?"

I bit my bottom lip, trying to keep from grinning.

I couldn't believe Triple T was asking me out. I decided to play it cool.

"I already have plans," I said, "but why don't you catch me next week?"

"I can do that," he agreed. "Why don't you give me your phone number and I'll call you so we can hook up."

I rattled off my number and he pulled out his Black-Berry and punched it in. I could hear a phone ringing through his earpiece, and then I heard someone answer.

"Hey, Jasmine. This is T. I'll call you later," Triple T said.

"What are you doing?" I asked in amazement.

He looked at me and winked. "Thank you," he said a few seconds later. "I just wanted to make sure you had given me your real number. I didn't want to have to track you down next week."

I laughed.

"Look, I gotta get out of here, but it was really good meeting you. I'll call you next week."

"Okay," I said.

"Yo, who was that clown stepping to you?" Kyle asked as we drove home.

"Boy, for a guy who wants to be in music, you

know absolutely nothing," Loretta said from the backseat. "That was Triple T."

Kyle shrugged. "What did he want?" he asked.

"Nothing that concerns you," I said.

Kyle opened his mouth like he was about to say something, but Loretta cut him off.

"Triple T looks even better in person than he does on TV. You think he'll call me?"

Probably not, I thought, remembering his promise to call me. "Girl, who knows? You know how celebrities are—always got something going on."

"Yeah, that's true," she said. She pulled a flask from her purse and took a sip. "Want some?"

I looked at her in my rearview mirror like she was crazy. "No, I don't want any. Where'd you get that?" I asked.

"Don't worry about it," she said, taking another sip. "That's just more for me."

By the time I had dropped Kyle and Loretta off, I was exhausted. I pulled my car into the garage so I wouldn't have to unload my equipment, and I headed straight to my room, glad that the house was quiet. I was a bit surprised that Mama or Derrick hadn't waited up for me, but I was a little relieved, too. I lay in bed for what seemed like hours, replaying my meeting with Triple T. There was something about him that I really liked, and as I drifted off to sleep, I was hoping that he really liked me, too.

chapter 6

Although I knew Triple T would call me, it surprised me when my phone rang Monday morning.

"Hello," I said, still half-asleep.

"Good morning," a male voice said.

"Kyle, why are you calling me so early?" I complained.

"Is Kyle your man?" the voice asked.

All at once I was wide awake, and I realized that the person on the other end sounded nothing like Kyle. "Who is this?" I asked, already suspecting it was Triple T.

"Oh, you've forgotten me already?" he teased.

I wanted to laugh, but instead I said, "If you don't tell me who this is right now, I'm hanging up. I don't have time for games."

He grew quiet for a second. "Well, excuse me," he said. "It's Terrence."

"I don't know anyone named Terrence," I said. By then I was grinning so hard my lips were almost touching my ears.

"Oh, it's like that?" he said. "Girl, this is Triple T."

"Oh, hey," I said. I sat up in bed and glanced at the clock. It was only nine in the morning.

"Can you at least pretend to be happy to hear from me?" he joked.

"Boy, you are so silly," I said.

"So what do you have up for the day?" he asked.

I shrugged, then remembered he couldn't see me. "Not much," I said, and it occurred to me as soon as the words were out of my mouth that I didn't want him to think I didn't have a life. "I'll probably just chill until my brother gets home from work and then see if he wants to work on our performance for All-City."

"Yeah, I heard you guys did a really good job at All-District."

"You know how we do," I joked.

He laughed. "Would you like to hang out with me? I have to go into the studio today to lay some tracks. If you'd like you can come with me and then we can do something afterward."

"Okay," I said, not concerned about sounding too excited. I had never been in a studio before, and I wasn't going to miss this chance. "Where do you want me to meet you?"

"I'm very impressed," he said.

"Why?" I said.

"You don't want me to come to your house for our first date. That's good."

"I don't know you," I said with an attitude.

"I know. Never let a strange man come to your house before you get to know him. You could be dealing with a psycho."

"Okay," I said, impressed with the fact that he was keeping it real.

"Why don't you meet me in Manhattan at Hit Makers around noon?"

"Cool," I said, already at my closet trying to figure out what to wear.

I decided to take the train into the city, and I spent the commute trying to imagine what it would be like to be in a real studio. On TV it seemed like there was always a party going on, with crowds of people talking loud, laughing, smoking, drinking and just having a good time.

Turned out that was the reality, too.

When Triple T met me at the front door of Hit

Makers, he greeted me with a friendly hug and a kiss on the cheek. "Welcome to Hit Makers," he said.

"Thanks," I said, looking around. The place was only about three stories high. We rode the elevator to the top floor, and when the doors opened, we walked down a short hall and stopped in front of a door. When Triple T opened it, smoke slapped me in my face. It only took a second for me to identify the pungent odor as weed. I wrinkled my nose.

"I'm not going in there," I said, stepping back.

He just laughed. "I thought you wanted to be in the music business."

"I do," I said.

"What do you think your studio sessions are going to be like?"

I thought about what he said and realized he was right. He allowed me to enter the room first, and although I took in the chicken bones and empty liquor bottles, my main focus was on the people. There were three celebrities in the room who currently had top ten Billboard songs. My mouth dropped open and Triple T laughed.

"I thought I'd surprise you," he whispered in my ear, and grinned.

I just smiled and tried to pretend I was used to hanging out with celebrities.

I took a seat on a low sofa and just chilled as I watched Triple T do his thing. I had to admit, I was really impressed. He reminded me a lot of myself, and it was obvious the artists respected him.

Just as I was really getting into things, my cell phone rang, and I knew by the ring tone it was Loretta.

"Hey, girl," I said.

"What are you doing?" she asked.

I was just about to tell her the truth when I changed my mind, because I knew she would try to come to the studio. "Just chilling with some friends."

"It sounds like you're at a party," she said.

I looked at all the action going on and grinned. "Something like that," I said evasively.

"Can you talk?" she asked.

I glanced at Triple T and he was really into what he was doing, so I figured I had a few minutes for my girl. "Yeah," I said. "What's up?"

"I've decided to get breast implants," she said proudly.

"What?" I screamed.

Triple T looked at me curiously, but I just smiled to let him know everything was okay. I got up and asked someone where the restroom was, then headed in there so I could have a little privacy.

"Have you lost your mind?" I screamed at Loretta before the bathroom door even closed.

"Girl, why are you trippin'?"

"First of all, you're only sixteen, and second, someone will be cutting on your body." She was silent for a minute. "Aren't those surgeries expensive?"

"Yeah, and?"

"So where are you getting the money for it?"

"I have a little saved," she said defensively. "My mom said she would take out a loan for the rest."

"You have got to be kidding me," I muttered. "Your mom is actually going to take out a loan so you can get some breasts?"

"Yeah," Loretta said.

I just shook my head. "What made you decide to do this?"

"I've been noticing on my job that most of the models being hired have implants. I think it will really boost the number of jobs I get."

I just sighed. I didn't understand Loretta, and it was obvious her mind was made up. "What do you need me to do?"

"I scheduled the surgery for next week. Can you pick me up afterward?"

"How are they able to fit you in so fast? Don't you need consultations or something?"

"I've already done all that stuff. I wasn't supposed to have it done until next month, but they had a cancellation. So can you pick me up?"

"Yes," I said grudgingly.

"Cool," she said. "I'll call you early next week and give you all the info."

"Okay," I said, and we hung up.

I spent the next twenty minutes thinking about my conversation with Loretta. It had really messed up my day at the studio. Triple T must have sensed something was going on, because he came over to me.

"You okay?" he asked.

I just nodded.

He grabbed my hand and led me out into the hall. "Hey, what's going on?" he asked.

"My friend Loretta—you remember, the one from the club?—she just told me about something she's planning to do, and it's got me tripping," I said.

"Do you want to talk about it?" he asked.

"Not really," I said.

He nodded. "Well, if you change your mind, know that you can talk to me. Okay?"

I looked down at the floor and nodded. He lifted my chin, forcing me to look at him. "Okay?" he said.

"Okay," I agreed.

He smiled. "I think I know something that might make you feel better."

"What?" I asked. His chocolate-brown eyes had me mesmerized.

"How'd you like to take a spin in the studio?"

"Are you serious?" I asked.

"Of course," he said. "Maybe we can do a little demo for you."

"Okay," I agreed, not even bothering to hide my excitement. "When do you want to do it?"

"How about now?" he asked.

"No problem," I said. Thousands of beats rushed through my head, but I decided to just go with the flow and spin it like that.

When I stepped into the studio for the first time, I felt as though I had come home. I took my place behind the mixer and Triple T gave me this dope beat, and as always, something came over me and I started vibing with the music. When I was done, I looked up to find everyone in the room staring at me.

"Yo, that was hot," said Mocha Love. Her record had been number one on the Billboard top ten for the last couple of weeks. "Yo, T, we gotta put her on the single."

I grinned as I looked at T.

"You want to do it?" he asked.

"Duh," I said before I realized how childish I sounded.

"Okay, we'll get some contracts in place and talk money and see if we can get Jasmine back in here next week," he said to Mocha Love.

She shook her head. "Man, the vibe is in here tonight. Can't we worry about all that legal stuff later and lay the track now?"

Triple T was about to say something, but I cut him off. "It's cool," I said. "We can do it tonight and I'll sign whatever. You don't even have to pay me. I'm just honored that these guys would ask me to be on their single."

Triple T looked at me and frowned before walking over to me. "Excuse us," he said to the room, and grabbed my hand. He led me outside again. "Don't do that," he said.

"Do what?" I asked, not having a clue what he was talking about.

"I know all this is cool and everything, but this is business, and we do things the right way, which means we get you a contract and your money."

"But I'm serious. You don't have to worry about paying m—"

"Jas," he said, "this single is going to be a hit. Do you know how much money you can make for being on this album?"

"But money isn't everything," I said, and suddenly my brother's face popped into my head. "Think about the kind of exposure I'll get from doing this. That's something money can't buy."

He shook his head. "We're going to do this the right way," he said. "I'll let you record with them tonight since everyone's here, but nothing gets released until the paperwork is in order. Deal?"

"Deal," I agreed.

We headed back to the studio, and Triple T gave the nod that we could continue. Everyone took their places, and we got to work. By the time we left, the sun was coming up. I looked at my watch and saw that it was six o'clock in the morning. Although being in the studio had left me feeling alive, my gut was telling me that once my mother got ahold of me, I was dead.

chapter 7

My heart dropped when I saw a police car sitting in front of my house. I seriously thought about having Triple T drive past my house and never coming back, but I knew that wasn't cool.

"You want me to come in?" he asked.

"Nah, it's okay," I said, hoping my voice didn't sound as shaky as it seemed to me.

"You sure?" he said, eyeing the police car.

I gave a hoarse laugh. "Boy, quit tripping. It's fine," I said.

He sighed and shook his head. "I'll call you later to check on you," he said.

I smiled and nodded.

When I walked through the door, my daddy was sitting slumped over in a chair, tears pouring down his face as though he had lost his best friend.

Derrick was the first one to spot me, and there was relief even on his face. "Thank God," he said, running over to me, but Mama got there first. She gathered me in her arms and stroked my hair.

"I was so worried," she said, stepping back so she could look at me. "Are you okay?"

I nodded, too stunned at how they were all reacting to speak.

"Where have you been?" Daddy asked, stepping forward to hug me.

I opened my mouth, but before I could say anything, Mama wrinkled her nose and frowned. "What is that smell?" she asked.

I looked around, trying to figure out what she was talking about.

She stepped toward me, grabbed a handful of my shirt and sniffed. "Have you been smoking weed?" she asked.

Before I could respond, she hauled off and slapped me so hard I thought she had knocked out a few of my teeth. I grabbed my stinging jaw and looked at her through watery eyes, wanting nothing more than to slap her back, but I wasn't that grown—or that stupid.

"We've been up all night worried sick about you and you come in here smelling like weed?" she asked, incredulous.

"But I can explain," I finally managed to say.

"It better be a good reason," Mama said, and if I hadn't already known I was in serious trouble, her tone proved it.

"I met this producer the other night, and he invited me to go to the studio with him yesterday," I said, getting excited at the memory despite my mother's anger. "There were some Billboard artists there, and they let me record with them. I'm going to have a song on the radio in a few weeks."

I glanced over at Daddy, and he looked excited, but he tried to play it off. Derrick looked happy, too, so, knowing I had them both on my side, I turned to Mama.

"I was vibing so hard with the music I didn't realize how late it was," I said. "Mama, I'm so sorry. I promise you it will never happen again."

Mama just laughed and shook her head. "I've been up all night wondering if you were lying on the side of the road hurt or even dead, and you tell me that you've been in a studio all night recording some song? Then you come strolling in here at seven o'clock in the morning and all you have to say is I'm sorry, it won't happen again?"

"But Mama, I'm going to have a song on the radio, and I'm going to get paid for it," I said.

"And I'm supposed to be impressed by that?" she asked.

I turned to Daddy. "Daddy, I promise it won't happen again," I said.

Daddy turned to Mama. "Baby, can't we cut her some slack this time?" he said. "She made a mistake. It won't happen again."

"You're right. It won't happen again," she agreed. She turned and looked at me. "Give me your car keys."

"What?" I exclaimed.

"Did I stutter?" she asked. "Give me your car keys."

"No," I said, taking a step back.

"No?" she repeated as though she hadn't heard me.

"No," I said again with attitude. "I paid for that car with my own money, and you can't take it from me."

"I don't care if you paid for it with blood, little girl. You don't run my house. Hand over the keys—now."

"No," I repeated.

"If you are living in my house, you will play by my rules," she said, getting up in my face.

"Then I just won't live in your house," I said, thinking about the money I had saved. "I'll get my own place."

I didn't even wait for her to respond. I went to my room and started packing my stuff up while Daddy and Derrick pleaded with me to stop. As I went back and forth to my car, stuffing it with everything I could, Mama calmly sat on the sofa flipping through the television channels. I kept waiting for her to try and stop me, but she never said a word.

When I realized I couldn't fit anything else in my car, I turned to Daddy and said, "I'll be back to get the rest of my things."

He pulled me outside. "Baby, what are you doing?" he asked. "Your mama's just mad right now. Give her a couple of hours to cool off."

"It's okay, Daddy. This has been coming for a long time," I said. "She's never supported my music."

I gave him a big hug and smiled to reassure him that I was going to be fine; then I looked at my brother, who seemed as though he was in shock trying to take everything in. "I'll call you," I said.

He just nodded.

I got in my car and drove away, watching my rearview mirror the entire time as I waited for Mama to come running after me.

The truth was I had no idea where I was going.

All kids think about running away at one time or another, but the reality was quite different than anything I'd ever dreamed. Since I was only sixteen, no one wanted to rent to me, so I ended up crashing at Loretta's. Her mother didn't have a problem charging me five hundred dollars a month to sleep on the living room sofa, but it was cool since I knew she was never home, so Loretta and I were able to come and go as we pleased.

I had been there a few days when Loretta woke me up early one morning.

"You ready?" she asked.

"Ready for what?" I said, picking up my watch to see what time it was.

"To take me to the hospital," she said, sounding excited.

"Hospital?" I said, not having a clue what she was talking about.

"Remember I asked you last week about picking me up after my breast surgery?" she said.

"Oh, yeah," I said, recalling the conversation.

"I figured since you're here, you might as well drive me there, too," she said.

"You're really going through with that?" I said.

"Yeah," she said, looking annoyed that I had even asked the question. "Hurry up and get dressed so we can go."

I had never seen Loretta look so determined. I sighed and pushed the covers off so I could get ready.

It didn't take me long to shower and throw on some clothes. As we drove into Manhattan—something Mama didn't like me to do—Loretta talked the entire way about all the gigs she was going to get thanks to her new breasts. It was still early, so there wasn't much traffic, which was a good thing. Loretta was about to drive me crazy.

Once we got to the hospital, Loretta signed in, and her name was called a few minutes later. She turned to me and smiled. "Say goodbye to my two little friends," she joked.

I just shook my head, still surprised that she was going through with this. "Good luck," I said.

She smiled and waved, and then she was gone.

I tried watching TV for a while, but it wasn't holding my attention, so I finally got up to go get something to eat.

When my phone rang, I thought it was Triple T or Derrick, who both called me every morning, but I didn't recognize the number on my caller ID.

"Hello," I said.

"This Jazzy J?" a voice asked.

"Yeah," I said. "Who's this?"

"My name's Jeremy. I got your number from Loretta. She said you deejay parties."

"Yeah," I said.

"I'm doing this little set for my twenty-first birthday, and I wanna hire you. How much you charge?"

Since I had started working with DC, I figured I could get away with charging more.

"How long do you want me to play?" I asked.

"My party's gon' last the whole weekend," he said, "and I want you here the entire time."

I laughed under my breath because I knew if he agreed to my rate I was about to get paid. "It'll be five grand," I said.

"Cool," he said.

"I need half of that up front," I said.

"Not a problem."

"When is the party?"

He gave me the dates, and I realized it was a couple of weeks after the All-City competition.

"So where you want me to send the money?" he asked.

I gave him Loretta's address, and he said he'd drop a check in the mail that day.

Pain was etched on Loretta's face when she was wheeled out of the recovery room. I glanced at her chest, and her breasts looked huge—three times as big as the 38D she wore before.

"You okay?" I asked.

She nodded weakly.

"Come on. Let's get you home," I said. I went to get the car and loaded Loretta inside.

"I didn't think it would hurt," she said quietly when we were halfway to Queens.

"It'll get better," I said, trying to comfort her.

She just stared out the window.

By the time I got Loretta settled, I was exhausted. I fell asleep still dressed, and when I woke up, there was so much sleep crusting my eyes that I couldn't open them. After washing my face, I went to check on Loretta.

She was sitting up in bed, flipping through a magazine.

"Hey, girl," I said. "How are you feeling?"

"A little better," she said with a small smile.

"Good," I said. "Do you need anything?"

She shook her head and winced. "No, thank you," she said.

"Have you eaten?" I asked.

"I'm not really hungry," she said.

"You've gotta eat something," I said.

I went to the kitchen and made some bacon and eggs along with some toast, then fixed two plates and two glasses of orange juice and carried them on a tray back to Loretta's room.

We were in the middle of eating when I heard my cell phone ringing. I hurried to the living room and rooted around in the sofa trying to find it before it went to voice mail. I didn't get it in time, so I checked my voice mail and was surprised to find I had several messages—two from Triple T, one from my brother and another from Kyle.

I didn't bother listening to my brother's or Kyle's messages, but I played Triple T's a few times.

"Hey, Jasmine. It's T," the first one began. "I just wanted you to know I was thinking about you. I hope you're having a great day."

I smiled as I saved the message, then hit the button to play the next one.

"Jas, it's T again. If you don't have plans tomorrow, I thought you might want to hang out. Give me a call."

A grin exploded across my face. I thought about calling him back, but I wanted to play it cool so he wouldn't know how much I was really feeling him.

I called my brother instead.

"Hey," he said when he realized it was me. "I just wanted to check on you."

"I'm okay," I said. "What's going on with you?"

"Nothing. Just working," he said. "What are you doing today?"

"Probably just hanging out with a friend," I said, another smile coming to my face.

"What friend?" Derrick asked suspiciously.

"His name's Nonya," I said.

"Nonya?" he repeated. "What kind of name is that?"

"Nonya business," I said, and burst out laughing.

It took him a second to catch my joke, but then I heard him chuckling. "That is so corny and old," he said.

"But you fell for it," I replied.

"Do you want to hang out after I get off work?" he asked.

"Yeah, that'll be cool," I said. "We need to practice for All-City. The competition's only a month away." I had finally convinced him a few days earlier to perform with me one final time.

"Are you coming over to the house?" he asked hopefully.

I shook my head and frowned; then I remembered he couldn't see me. "I'll pass," I said.

I hadn't been back to the house nor had I spoken to Mama since I left, and I really had no intention of doing either one.

"You know, Mama really misses you," Derrick said quietly. "I do, too."

I ignored his last statement. "Mama knows where to find me if she wants to get in touch with me," I said with an attitude.

"Jas, why don't you try being the bigger person?" he said.

"Whatever, Derrick," I said. "So are you coming over here or what?"

"Yeah, I'll be over around six," he said, sighing.

After we hung up, I called Kyle.

"You called me?" I asked.

"Yeah. I just hadn't talked to you in a while, and I wanted to see what's up. How are you doing?" he asked.

"I'm cool," I said.

"You still staying with Loretta?" he asked.

"Yeah," I snapped. What was it with everyone's interest in where I was staying?

"I was just asking," he said. "How's Loretta doing?"

"She's still in pain," I said.

"Maybe I'll come check on you guys later," he said.

"Okay. Derrick's coming over, too. We can hang out like old times," I said, suddenly missing that.

"I'll see you later," Kyle said.

I waited another twenty minutes before I called Triple T. I was a little disappointed when his voice mail picked up, but I left a message, then went to check on Loretta, who was asleep. I cleaned up the kitchen, then watched TV for a little while. I had just started to doze off when my cell phone rang. I knew by the tone it was Triple T, and I smiled.

"Hello," I said, trying to sound sexy and pretending I didn't know it was him.

"Hey, Jas," he said. His voice sent chills down my spine.

"Hey, T," I sang.

"What are you getting into today?" he asked.

"Nothing much," I said. "What about you?"

"I just finished a meeting, and I'm free the rest of the day."

I glanced at the clock. It was a little after ten. "You've already had a meeting this early in the morning?"

"Yeah," he said. "You never heard that saying 'the early bird catches the worm'?"

I just giggled.

"Have you eaten?" he asked.

I almost said yes, but then I changed my mind. "I was just about to get something," I said.

"Why don't we go together?" he said.

"Sounds good," I agreed.

He gave me an address and told me to meet him in an hour.

I was glad I had taken a bath the night before, so all I had to do was wash up and get dressed. I found a jean miniskirt, some leggings and a sexy black T-shirt and threw on my Air Force Ones; then I combed my hair and added a little lip gloss. I went to check on Loretta, who was still asleep, so I left her a note telling her that Derrick and Kyle were coming over and that I would be back later that afternoon.

I drove to the address Triple T had given me and curiously took in the brick building I pulled up to. It looked like a regular apartment building, and I wondered if there was a deli or something inside it where Triple T and I were going to eat.

I pushed through the main door and made my way to the security door, where I spotted a note.

Jasmine,
Ring the buzzer for 3B.
T

I did as requested, and was immediately buzzed into the building. I took the elevator upstairs, and when I got off, there was another note on 3B.

Let yourself in…

Again, I did as I was told. Soft music greeted me at the door. Although the sun was shining bright outside, I wasn't able to tell that inside, because the shades were drawn and the room was dark except for the candles glowing.

My mouth dropped open in surprise. I peered around the room, and I noticed Triple T standing next to a table laid out with enough food to feed the Times Square crowd on New Year's Eve.

We just stared at each other in silence for what felt like an eternity until T walked to me and kissed my cheek.

"Hi, beautiful," he said, and I blushed.

"Hey," I said. "What's all this?" I motioned toward the table.

"I told you we were going to have breakfast," he said.

He thought for a second. "Maybe I should have said brunch."

He smiled, and I felt my heart melt.

"This is so sweet," I said. "No one has ever done anything this nice for me."

"Good," he said, leading me to the table. He seated me, then seated himself.

"Did you cook all this?" I asked.

He hesitated for a moment, then laughed. "I

started to lie, but no. I had it catered. I wasn't sure what you liked, so I ordered a little of everything."

"There's no way I'll be able to eat all this," I said, taking in the food. It really looked like he had ordered the entire menu. There was shrimp cocktail on a bed of ice, a whole lobster, steak, bacon, sausage, scrambled eggs, pancakes and waffles, bagels with smoked salmon, hash browns and a lot of food I had never seen before.

"This all looks really good," I said.

"Help yourself," he said.

I was too nervous to eat in front of him, but I didn't want to offend him, especially after he had gone to the trouble of ordering all the food.

I took a few shrimp and some scrambled eggs, and T helped himself to a little of everything. I nibbled on my food, while he dug in like he hadn't eaten in days.

The food was incredible, and I quickly went back for seconds. I decided to be a little more adventurous and tried some crêpes suzette and eggs Benedict, as well as some bacon.

"So how's your friend Loretta?" he finally asked.

"She's okay. I still can't believe she got implants," I said, shaking my head.

"A lot of women do," he said.

"Yeah, but she's so young. I feel bad that she felt the pressure to do that. Besides, they turned out horrible—one is way bigger than the other." I gave a sad smile.

"What's going on at home?" he asked.

"The same thing. My mother and I still aren't speaking," I said.

He shook his head and frowned. "You need to apologize," he said.

"Are you serious?" I asked. I looked at him and realized that he was.

"Family is important," he said. "Nobody is going to have your back like your mama. Even if she was wrong, you need to apologize."

I rolled my eyes.

"I'm serious," he said. "Promise me you'll at least think about it."

"Okay," I agreed.

I looked around the room, finally taking everything in. Even in the dark, I could tell the space was amazing. It was huge, which wasn't normally the case with places in New York—except the ones you saw on TV—and there was lots of expensive furniture, and a plasma-screen TV hanging over the fireplace.

I got up from the table and walked over to the

windows, which were covered with heavy drapes. I pulled one aside and sunlight came spilling in. I looked out on the most amazing view of Manhattan.

"Whose place is this?" I asked, turning around. I jumped a little when I realized T was right behind me.

"It's mine," he said.

"For real?" I asked, impressed. I was trying not to let on how my heart was slamming into my chest at his nearness. "How long have you lived here?"

"A couple of years," he said.

"You've been here since you were seventeen?" I asked.

He shrugged like it was no big deal. "Yeah," he said.

"Do you live here by yourself?"

"Of course."

"I tried getting my own place," I said thoughtfully, "but no one would rent to me."

"That's because you didn't show them enough money," he said. "The same thing happened to me. I ended up just buying the building."

"You own this building?" I asked in amazement.

He shrugged again. "Yeah. This one and a few others."

"How much money do you have?" I let the question slip before I realized how rude it was to ask. "Sorry. I know that's none of my business."

He just laughed. "I've done pretty well for myself," he said. "I have a few million in the bank."

"Wow," I said. I'd thought I was doing well because I had managed to save a few thousand.

"Can you help me get my own place?" I asked.

He nodded. "But you have to promise me that you'll make up with your mama," he said, taking a step closer to me. "Do you promise?"

At that moment, I would have agreed to fly to the moon by flapping my arms. "Yes," I breathed.

Although I was expecting it, it still came as a pleasant surprise when his lips met mine. The kiss only lasted a couple of seconds, but it was the best I'd ever had, which maybe wasn't saying a lot since I'd only kissed two other boys.

"How much money do you have?" he asked.

I told him, and he turned thoughtful. "Keep saving," he said. "This business is crazy—you don't know when you'll be out of work. I'll also have you talk to my man about investing. I'll talk to my housing man today about hooking you up with a place."

I was about to tell him that I didn't have enough

money to buy a house or a building, but he stopped me. "I'll front you the money," he said.

I opened my mouth to protest but he held up his hand, stopping me. "It's cool," he said. "People know me, and even if they don't respect me, they respect my bank account. Always remember, Jas, that with the right amount of money, you can get anything you want."

chapter 8

Triple T and I spent the rest of the day just hanging out, getting to know each other.

He told me he had a younger sister my age who lived in Atlanta with his parents. He had been in New York for almost three years, and also owned a house in Atlanta, as well as one in L.A. He had his attorney come over; we finalized the contract for my work on Mocha Love's single, and he let me hear the version of it that would be released to radio stations.

I knew I was good at what I did, but I exceeded even my own expectations.

Over dinner, Triple T asked me about my other musical interests.

"I heard you can rap," he said, wiping his mouth with a napkin.

I had gotten over my nervousness about eating in

front of him, so I nodded, since I had a mouthful of the best cheeseburger I had ever tasted. Once I'd swallowed, I said, "Yeah, I can do a little something." I grinned at him, and he smiled and reached over and scraped something from my teeth. I started blushing when he held up a piece of lettuce for my inspection.

"I am so embarrassed," I said, covering my face.

"Don't be," he said. "I just want you to know I've always got your back, okay?"

I nodded, still looking at the floor.

"Hey," he said, lifting my chin. "Always know you can be yourself around me. You never have to be embarrassed or scared to say anything to me. Your spunkiness and outspokenness is one of the first things that attracted me to you."

"You're attracted to me?" I asked, looking into his eyes.

"No doubt," he said. He leaned over and gave me a tiny kiss on the cheek, and I smiled. "So, let me hear you rap."

I grinned and cleared my throat before freestyling for him. By the time I was done, he was shaking his head.

"What's wrong?" I asked, thinking he didn't like it.

"That was hot," he said. "I'm impressed."

"Thank you," I said.

"When your album comes out, it's going to be crazy," he said. "You know I'm going to produce it for you, right? I already got some ideas."

"You'd produce my album?" I said.

"No doubt. Why wouldn't I produce my girl's album?"

My heart slammed into my chest when he called me his girl. I got excited until I remembered that people said that all the time. I had called Loretta that more times than I cared to remember, and I knew I wasn't trying to get with her.

I suddenly realized I hadn't checked on my friend. I pulled out my cell phone and called her, but she didn't pick up, so I figured she was still sleeping. I thought about leaving a message, but I figured I would see her in a few hours, so there wasn't any point. She would be able to tell from the caller ID that I had called.

Triple T had made his way over to the piano in his living room during my call, so I followed him.

"Do you play?" I asked.

"Of course," he said, and picked out a tune. "Do you?"

"I can do a little something," I said.

He grabbed my hand and pulled me down so I was sitting between his legs. "Show me," he whispered in my ear.

Chills ran down my spine.

I began playing an old-school tune, trying to ignore the trail of kisses he was running down my neck. At one point he snuck a real kiss, and I stopped my playing to return it. It seemed to last for about five minutes, and my body was on fire.

Triple T was making his way toward my breasts when reality set in. "Stop," I said, pushing him away.

"What's the matter?" he asked. His voice sounded really deep and sexy, and I gulped.

"We have to stop," I said.

"Why?"

"Because I just met you." I tugged at my shirt and tried to move away from him, but he held me firm.

"So? You know you want me as much as I want you," he whispered, placing another kiss on my neck.

"T, that's not the point. I'm still a virgin," I said softly.

"Oh." He nodded in understanding before kissing me on my forehead. "You know, Jasmine, your honesty is one of the things I love most about you."

"You love me?" I said in amazement.

He looked deeply into my eyes before he said, "I love you." Between each word, he gently placed a kiss on different parts of my face.

"But you just met me," I said.

"That doesn't change how I feel," he said.

I smiled. I had been feeling the same thing, but I was too scared to admit it. I had heard people talking about love at first sight, but I'd never thought it would happen to me. "I love you, too," I said.

He grinned, then turned serious. "I want you to know there's no pressure on my end. When you decide you're ready to take our relationship to the next level, just let me know," he said. I nodded. "In the meantime, I think I'd better move."

It took me a second to understand why. I had been trying to ignore his bulge pressing into my side, but when he stood, it was hard to ignore. I couldn't believe I had done that to him.

"You okay?" I asked softly.

"Yeah, I'll be fine," he said. "It's nothing a cold shower won't cure. I'll be back in a few minutes." He gave me another kiss and then disappeared into his master bedroom, which he had shown me earlier. Inside was a marble-tiled bathroom complete with heated floors, a Jacuzzi big enough to swim in, a glass-enclosed shower and a sauna.

Figuring he might be a while, I started playing around on the piano. After a few minutes the words to a new song came to mind. I looked around for some paper, kicking myself for having forgotten my notebook, but I didn't see any. I did spy a digital tape recorder. I hit Record and just lost myself in the music. The words and melody just flowed, and when I finished I was drained.

"That was amazing," Triple T said quietly once I was done.

"How long have you been standing there?" I asked.

"Long enough," he said. "Why didn't you tell me you could sing and that you could write?"

"I was going to," I said, "but we got preoccupied. I hope you don't mind, but I used your recorder."

"Not at all," he said. "Anything I have is yours. What good is having things if I can't share them with the woman I love?"

I blushed. "Thank you," I said simply.

"No, thank you," he said.

"What are you thanking me for?"

"For just being you," he said. He stared at me for a few seconds, and I felt myself becoming self-conscious. I rubbed my hair.

"What?" I said.

"I've never met anyone like you, and I don't want you to get away. Jasmine, will you be my girlfriend?"

I felt my heart melt. I thought about asking if he was sure, but I could tell by the way he was looking at me that he was. "Yes," I said, and threw myself into his arms. We stood there grinning at each other.

"We should go out and celebrate," he said.

"Okay," I agreed. "Where are we going?"

"Let's get some ice cream."

"Cool."

He made a call; then he grabbed my hand and we headed downstairs. Right in front of his building was a black-on-black Cadillac Escalade that was so shiny I could see my reflection, even though it was dusk.

"Is this yours?" I asked, when a man got out of the driver's seat and held the back door open for us.

"Yeah, one of them," he said, as though everyone had more than one car.

"How many do you have?" I asked, looking around the interior. There were television monitors in the headrests, along with a DVD player and PlayStation 3. I sank back in my seat and thought I had never felt anything so soft in my life.

"Twenty," he said.

I turned and looked at him. "You have twenty cars?" I asked incredulously.

"Yeah," he said. "Tomorrow we can go get you one. I can't have my girl riding around in some beat-up old car."

I looked at him and rolled my neck. "My car is not beat-up," I said.

"Okay," he said, "but I'm still buying you a new one."

"No, you're not," I said. "I appreciate what you're trying to do, but I make my own money, and when I decide to get a new car, it will be because I'm paying for it. Besides, you've already said you're gonna give me the money to buy a place—"

His kiss stopped me. Just as I was getting into it, the car stopped, and he pulled away. "We'll talk about this later," he said.

"Okay," I agreed, too breathless to say anything else.

We went into Cold Stone Creamery and each got huge waffle cones. I had never been there before, but I knew I would quickly become addicted. They used homemade ice cream and made any combination with mix-ins right before your eyes. I decided on the cake batter ice cream with brownie, Oreo cookies and caramel, and Triple T got cake batter with Snickers, Oreos and peanut butter. It sounded nasty, but it actually tasted pretty good.

As we ate, the workers sang several ice cream songs to the tune of different nursery rhymes. It was actually kind of cute. At one point, Triple T made up a beat, and I freestyled. We had the whole place, which was packed, rocking, and received a standing ovation.

Once we were done, Triple T got a pint of our special creations to go; then, we hopped back into his Escalade where his driver, Manny, had been patiently waiting.

"Where to?" Triple T asked.

I shrugged. "What time is it?" I asked.

He glanced at his diamond-encrusted watch. "Ten o'clock," he said.

"Are you serious?" I grabbed his wrist to check the time for myself. When I saw he was telling the truth, I groaned. "Oh, man, my brother is going to kill me."

"Why?" Triple T asked.

"I was supposed to meet him and Kyle at Loretta's hours ago." I searched for my purse so I could get my cell phone and call him, but I remembered I'd left it at Triple T's house.

"Let's head over there now," Triple T suggested. He unhooked his BlackBerry from his belt loop and handed it to me. "Call them and tell them we're on our way," he said.

"You don't mind?" I asked, already punching in the number.

"Why would I?" he said. "It gives me a chance to meet the people you love most in the world and to spend some time with you."

Loretta answered the phone on the second ring. "Girl, where you at?" she asked, sounding more like herself.

"I've been hanging with—" I glanced at Triple T "—my boyfriend," I said, and grinned, loving the way that sounded.

"What?" Loretta screamed. "When did you get a man? Wait a second." She came back to the phone almost immediately. "Jas, why does my caller ID say this is Terrence Thomas's number?"

"Because it is," I said simply.

"Terrence Thomas as in Triple T?" she asked, not waiting for me to answer. "Triple T is your man? Since when?"

I shook my head. "We'll talk about it later," I said. "Are Derrick and Kyle still there?"

"Yeah, they were just getting ready to leave. We've called you like five times. Now I understand why you didn't answer."

"Tell them we'll be there in a few minutes," I said.

"Cool. Wait a minute. Did you say 'we'? We who?"

"You'll see," I sang.

I was just about to hang up when I heard Loretta say, "Jas, you better not be bringing Triple T over here with me all bandaged up. I'm going to kill you."

I just laughed. "See you later, Loretta," I said, and hung up.

"Maybe we should take your peeps some food," he suggested.

"Good idea," I said. Even if they had already eaten, I figured they wouldn't be able to resist. Triple T phoned in an order to a local pizza joint and was told the food would be ready in five minutes. I had never had service that fast.

"How'd you manage that?" I asked.

"I told you, the right amount of money will buy you anything," he said.

When we arrived at Loretta's, Kyle and Derrick were stretched out on the sofa, which doubled as my bed. As usual, Loretta's mother was nowhere to be found.

"Hey, guys," I said, putting the pizza on the coffee

table and walking over to give each of them a hug. "Where's Loretta?"

Derrick nodded toward her bedroom. "She muttered something about having to get dressed, then headed back there," he said. "Where've you been?" He looked beyond me at T and I turned to introduce them.

Derrick was polite enough, but Kyle was not impressed, especially when I said T was my boyfriend. He got up in T's face, looked him dead in the eye and told him, "If you hurt her, I will hurt you."

I had never seen Kyle behave that way. "Boy, you are so silly. Go sit down somewhere," I said, trying to play off his behavior.

T just stood there laughing. He looked like he was about to say something, but Loretta came switching into the room. "Hey, T," she said, giving him a big hug and linking her arm around his. "I'm glad you could make it."

She was talking as though she had personally invited him. I guess she was really feeling better. She had on this fitted shirt that barely covered her breasts, which were still bandaged, and these tight black pants that showed off more of her than I wanted to see. She had put on a long curly wig, which actually looked good on her.

"Hey, Loretta," I said.

"Oh, hey, girl," she said, not bothering to look at me. "So, T, can I get you anything?" She led him to the sofa and sat right up under him—an inch more and she would have been in his lap.

"Move, Loretta," I said, and for a second I thought she was going to ignore me.

I grabbed her arm and helped her to the other end of the sofa.

"Why you tripping?" she said. "I was just trying to make T feel at home."

"Whatever, Loretta," I said. I turned and looked at Derrick and Kyle. "You guys hungry?"

As expected, they didn't turn down the free food. We sat watching the end of the movie they were watching—well, everyone was watching but Kyle, who seemed to be staring T down.

After the movie was over, we sat around just looking at each other—or rather, Loretta was looking at T.

"What time is it?" Kyle finally asked.

I glanced at the clock on the cable box. "A little after midnight," I said.

Derrick stood and stretched. "I should be getting home," he said, trying to cover a yawn.

"Man, why you trippin'?" I asked. "You don't have to work tomorrow."

He looked at me and shook his head, and I remembered our curfew, which I hadn't had to follow since I'd moved out almost a month ago. "I forgot you still live at home with your mama," I said, laughing at my own joke.

Derrick was about to say something when Triple T jumped in. "Baby, that's not cool," he said. "You need to chill with that."

I didn't know whether to focus on the fact that he was calling me baby or that he had something to say to me in front of my friends.

T looked at Derrick. "I've been telling your sister that she needs to make up with your mom. Family is everything, man. She doesn't realize what she has."

I saw a level of respect light Derrick's eyes, which annoyed me for some reason.

"But I do realize you're talking about me like I'm not here," I snapped.

"Sorry, baby," T said, cupping my knee.

I grinned at him as I melted. "It's okay," I said. I had never had a guy pay me this much attention before, especially in front of my friends, and I loved it.

I glanced at his hand on my knee and felt my insides warm. When I looked at up, Kyle was staring straight at me looking like he wanted to chew cement.

"What?" I asked.

He shook his head, then changed his mind. "I need to talk to you—alone," he said.

"Whatever you can say to me, you can say to T," I said, linking our fingers together.

"No, I can't," Kyle said. He grabbed my arm and helped me up off the couch.

When I tried to pull away, he looked at me. "Five minutes," he said.

I looked at T. "It's cool," he said.

The minute we were in Loretta's room, I turned to face Kyle. "What is your problem?" I asked, placing my hands on my hips.

"Why are you with this clown?" he said. He was trying to keep his voice low, but I had a feeling T could hear everything he said.

"What are you talking about?" I said. "T's a good guy. He loves me, and I love him."

Kyle barked a laugh. "Jas, you can't be serious. You just met this dude. How are you gon' say you're in love with him?"

"Why do you care?" I asked. "It's none of your business."

He looked at me and closed the door to Loretta's

bedroom. "You are my business. You've been my girl for a long time, Jas, and I've always been real with you. I don't trust this guy. There's something about him I don't like."

I relaxed a little when I realized Kyle was just looking out for me. "You're just jealous," I teased.

"Maybe," he said.

"Don't worry, Kyle," I said, patting him on the shoulder. "You'll always be my boy. There's room in my heart to love both you and T." I went to open the bedroom door.

Kyle swung me around, pushed me up against the door and kissed me so hard I lost my breath. Before I realized it, I was kissing him back, grabbing at his clothes.

At the sound of a knock on the door, we sprang apart, chests heaving, and I looked at him in shock.

I smoothed my hair and tried to straighten my clothes as Kyle opened the door. Derrick took in the scene and grinned, although he didn't say anything except, "I'm leaving. I'll call you tomorrow, Jas."

I nodded, too embarrassed to speak.

Kyle headed back to the living room, giving me a few minutes to get myself together.

What just happened? I wondered, looking at myself in the mirror. Although my breathing had slowed down, my face was really red, and I looked…I looked like I had been thoroughly kissed.

When I finally felt as though I looked halfway normal, I returned to the living room to find Loretta once again sitting up under T.

"Girl, why are you up under my man?" I asked, avoiding looking at Kyle whose eyes I could feel on me.

"He was just telling me all about the music business," Loretta said. "T promised to introduce me to some of the people he knows. I just know he's going to be my big break."

I rolled my eyes.

T untangled himself from Loretta and stood. "Baby, I'm gonna head back home now," he said. He walked over to kiss me on the cheek. "I'll call you in the morning. I love you."

I stood on tiptoe and gave him a tiny kiss on the lips. "Call me when you get in so I know you made it home okay. I love you," I said, wrapping my arms around him, hoping Kyle would see just how devoted I was to my man.

T looked at Kyle and nodded; then he turned to Loretta, who was standing there like she was waiting on a kiss, as well. He touched her on the shoulder.

"I'll give you a call tomorrow," she said.

He just smiled.

"You gave her your number?" I asked T with an attitude.

He shook his head.

I turned to Loretta. "How are you going to call him?"

"Girl, I got his number off the caller ID." She grinned. "Bye, T."

I was about to walk him to the car, but he stopped me at the door. "It's okay, baby. You stay here and finish chilling with your friends."

"I'm sorry they were acting so crazy," I said.

"It's cool. I'm glad I got to hang out with them. It's good getting to know people who know you. Stay beautiful," he said, kissing me once again. Then he was gone.

When I made it back to the living room, Loretta was nowhere in sight.

"Where's Loretta?" I asked Kyle, still avoiding looking at him.

"She said she was tired and she was going to bed," he said, picking up the remote.

"That was fast," I said. "I guess all that acting wore her out. You're not leaving?"

"Nah," he said. "I figured I'd chill here for a

minute." He leaned back against the sofa pillows, making himself comfortable.

"That's cool, but you're sitting on my bed," I said. I was trying to keep our conversation as normal as possible, but my mind was racing as I tried to figure out what had happened in Loretta's bedroom.

He moved over to make room for me. "What, you're scared to sit next to me now?"

"Boy, please," I said, giving him a dry laugh. I plopped down next to him, and I glanced at him out of the corner of my eye as I pretended to watch some old Nick Cannon movie.

When had Kyle become so fine? I wondered. He used to be real skinny, but he had started working out the previous summer, and I realized he was cut. His mustache had finally come in, and it made him look much older and sexier. I shook myself, not believing that I was thinking this way about one of my closest friends.

"Do you plan on talking about what happened in there?"

"What do you mean?" I asked, playing dumb.

"Jas, don't trip," he said, throwing the remote on the couch and looking at me.

"Oh, you're talking about that little kiss? Boy, that wasn't nothing." I waved my hand at him and turned my attention back to the screen, but I saw him nod out of the corner of my eye.

He stroked his newly grown goatee thoughtfully. "It wasn't nothing, huh?"

I looked him dead in the eye so I could pretend I hadn't been affected by him. "No," I said with an attitude. "I don't know why you did that, anyway. You know I got a man."

"I did it because I want to be your man. I have for a long time," he said seriously.

I looked at him like he was crazy. "Boy, quit playing."

"Do I look like I'm playing?" he asked.

He didn't.

I turned to face the TV again. "Like I said, I have a man," I said.

"You weren't acting like you had one when you were kissing me a little while ago."

"First of all, I wasn't kissing you—"

That was as far as I got. Kyle had me on the sofa so fast, it took my mind a second to catch up with what was happening. When it registered, I was wrapped in his arms, kissing him with everything I had in me.

It was by far the best kiss I had ever had.

When Kyle finally ended the kiss, I just stared at him.

"We can't do this," I said.

"Why not?" he asked softly.

"T's my man."

"He doesn't have to be," Kyle said.

I thought about what he said. "But I want him to be," I said.

"Why? Because he's got money and connections?"

I nodded slowly. "That's part of it," I said. "I love him, too."

Kyle shook his head. "You love him, but you're sitting here on a sofa with me slobbing me down?"

I couldn't say anything, so I looked at the floor.

"Jas, you're my girl, and if you don't want to be with me, I'll respect that, but don't give me some bull reason for it. I've always had your back, and I always will. I'm telling you right now that T is up to no good. Think about it. He's almost twenty years old. What would he want with a sixteen-year-old girl other than sex?"

"The same thing you want," I threw back at him.

Kyle just laughed. He stood and walked to the front door, and without my consent, my body followed him. "Where are you going?" I asked.

He turned the doorknob, his back still to me. "The day is going to come when you realize who's really down with you. When you're ready, you know where to find me." He opened the door and walked out without looking back.

I just had to have the last word, so I screamed at him, "Don't flatter yourself, Kyle. My man loves me." Even as I said the words, I wondered if they were really true. This whole thing with T was happening so fast, and although I really believed he cared for me, I wasn't sure if it was love.

Kyle didn't even bother to respond as he got in his brand-new Toyota Prius, a graduation present from his mother, and drove off.

I headed to the bathroom and prepared for bed. As I was going to turn off the overhead light, I spotted a white envelope with my name and a return address handwritten on the front. Curious, I opened it and found a check for five thousand dollars from the guy who wanted me to deejay his party. I guess he was really serious about me being there, since he had paid the entire amount up front. I smiled, thinking about all the money I was making. It looked like I wouldn't need T to front me the money for a place after all, I realized, calculating all I'd made so far that summer.

When I finally turned off the overhead light and climbed onto the sofa, I lay awake for hours thinking about T and Kyle and wondering if it was possible to be in love with two men at the same time.

chapter 9

T and I had only been dating a few weeks, but we had become inseparable. I started meeting him at his house and different places around the city because Loretta was driving me crazy trying to get up under him, and every time I turned around, Kyle was at the house. I had stepped to Loretta a couple of times, but it didn't seem to have any effect, and I tried ignoring Kyle, but it was hard.

T was still helping me find a house, but we hadn't found one I liked yet, and I still refused to speak to my mother, so for the moment I was stuck with Loretta.

One night after T and I had had a movie marathon, watching movies that hadn't even made it to the theaters yet, T gave me one of the biggest surprises of my life. He grabbed my hand and pulled me out of my plush movie-theater-style chair and led me into his bedroom.

"Close your eyes," he said.

"T," I protested, "you know I hate surprises."

He just laughed, because he knew I was lying. Every time I was with him, he had something for me, and I loved it. "Hold out your hands and close your eyes," he ordered.

I did as he requested, and he placed what felt like a small box in my hands. "Open them," he said.

"What's this?" I asked, staring at the blue box with the white ribbon. Since hanging out with T, I had learned that it was the jewelry store Tiffany's signature box.

"Open it," he encouraged.

I pulled off the ribbon and removed the lid. Inside, on a bed of cotton, was a sterling-silver key chain shaped like a heart. "It's beautiful," I said. I stared into his eyes. "Thank you."

"It's so you can have a piece of my heart with you wherever you go," he said.

I threw my arms around his neck and kissed him. "I love you," I said, and immediately an image of Kyle came to mind, but I pushed it away.

"I love you, too," he said, and grinned.

"I'm going to put my keys on it right now," I

said, running to find the Coach purse he had given me the week before.

"Wait," he said, stopping me in my tracks. "Before you add those keys to it, there's another one I have for you." He reached into his pocket and pulled out a silver key.

"What's that to?" I asked.

"My house," he said.

I looked at him in amazement.

"Jas, you're over here all the time, and I want you to know that my door is always open to you. You can even move in if you'd like."

He saw the frown that covered my face and quickly said, "Or if you'd just like to come in here to chill to get away from your girl, that's cool, too."

"Thank you," I said, too stunned to say anything else. No man had ever made me feel this way.

"We really need to practice," I said to my brother the next day when he called me.

All-City was only a week away, and we had only worked on our routine once or twice, but I wasn't worried. Derrick and I always had our thing locked up, and I knew even if we only practiced one more time we were still going to win.

"Yeah, I've been meaning to talk to you about that," he said.

"What about it?" I asked, only half paying him attention. I was going through some albums for a party I had to do Saturday night.

"I've decided not to perform with you."

"What?" I yelled. I dropped the album I was holding, not caring about damaging it. "You can't be serious. I thought we were past that."

"Look, Jas, I've been thinking about this, and I've decided that I really want to focus on school—"

"But school doesn't start until after the competition," I interrupted.

"I know," he said, "but if you'll let me finish… Morgan is holding this Future Medical Leaders symposium next weekend, and I've decided to attend."

"But you promised," I whined.

"I know," he said softly. "I'm sorry."

I knew this symposium must have meant a lot to him for him to cancel on me, but I didn't care.

"What about our record deal?" I asked.

"You mean your record deal. You've always known that's not what I want to do. You're going to win the competition and land a deal without me. I think the real question is what you're going to do about school. You haven't said anything about it since you moved out. Are you still planning to go?"

"No," I said, shaking my head. "The only reason I was really considering it was because Mama and Daddy wanted it so bad, but since I'm not living at home anymore, that's not that big of a deal. It's not like I'm not making money."

Derrick sighed, and I could tell he wanted to say something, but he didn't, and I didn't push him.

"Look, I've got to go. Since you're not going to perform with me, I've got to call the organizers of the competition and let them know; then I've got to redo my routine." I was hoping I could make him feel guilty.

"Okay," he said, and hung up.

I took the phone from my ear and looked at it in amazement. Derrick had never hung up on me. I thought about calling him back, but I decided I'd just talk to him later.

I tried to remember what I'd done with the organizers' phone number. Derrick normally reminded me about such things, but I didn't want to call him to ask. It took me an hour to remember I had stored it in my phone.

The phone rang a couple of times before a female answered.

"Good morning. Image Records. This is Doris Jones. How may I help you?"

Her greeting threw me for a second. I hadn't been expecting someone from Image Records to answer the phone.

"Hello?" she said.

"Uh…hi, Ms. Jones. My name is Jasmine Richardson, and I'm one of the acts for All-City."

"Hi, Jasmine. You're performing with your brother, right? How may I help you?"

"How'd you know I was performing with my brother?" I asked curiously.

"It's my job to know," she said. "Besides, there are only five acts."

"Oh," I said, having forgotten that there was only going to be one act from each borough.

"How may I help you?" she repeated.

"My brother won't be able to participate," I said.

"Oh, dear," she said, and I could sense her frown through the phone.

"I'll still be there," I said quickly.

"Hang on for a minute," she said.

She put me on hold for about five minutes before she came back. "Jasmine, unfortunately, if your brother doesn't participate, then you won't be able to, either."

"What?" I screamed.

"You guys entered the first competition as a team, and you'll have to perform that way at All-City. It wouldn't be fair to the other teams if we let you make changes to your group."

"But I'm still planning to perform," I said.

"I understand, but rules are rules," she said firmly. "Should I contact the runner-up to replace you?"

I could just picture her with her finger poised over the phone keypad, ready to give someone else the chance to win my record deal. "No," I said, figuring I would just show up the day of the event without Derrick and rock it.

"Maybe I should give them notice," she said thoughtfully. "I wouldn't want you to come the day of the event and think you can bend the rules."

"I wouldn't do that," I protested, wondering if she had read my mind.

"So you and your brother will be performing?" she said.

"Yes," I said, realizing that I had to convince Derrick to perform with me one last time.

After getting off the phone with Ms. Jones, I jumped in my car and headed over to my parents' house. I had only been back once since I'd left, and that was only long enough to collect the rest of my things.

Derrick was in the driveway working on his car.

"We need to talk," I said the minute I pulled up behind him.

He didn't look surprised to see me.

He put down his wrench and turned to me. "What do we need to talk about?" he said.

"You've got to perform with me," I said. "They won't let me perform otherwise."

He took his time wiping his hands on an oily cloth before responding. "I told you there's a symposium the same weekend."

"I know," I said. "Derrick, I promise you I tried to set it up so I could perform on my own, but they won't let me. If you don't do it, I guess I'll just have to sign with DC."

I figured this would get him, because despite all the money DC had paid me, Derrick still couldn't stand him.

"Jasmine, stop with the games," he said.

"What are you talking about?" I asked innocently.

He just shook his head. "Grow up," he said. "I told you, the world does not revolve around you. Other people have dreams, too. You were woman enough to move out of this house, now be woman enough to stop playing games and just ask for my help."

I thought about saying something smart, but it wasn't the time. "Fine," I finally said. "If you could perform with me one last time, I would really appreciate it. I promise I won't ask for anything else."

"Yes, you will," he said. "You wouldn't be Jasmine if you didn't come begging to me for something." He grinned, and I picked up a rag and threw it at him.

"Thanks, Derrick," I said, giving him a hug. "What are you going to do about your symposium?"

"I realized after I talked to you on the phone that it's the following weekend," he said, and turned back to his car.

"So you put me through all that for nothing?"

He shrugged. I looked around for something else to throw at him. I spotted the hose, which gave me a much better idea. I picked it up and made sure it was turned all the way up.

"Derrick," I yelled.

"What?" he said, sounding annoyed. He leaned in to the backseat of his car without bothering to look at me.

"Can we practice once you're done?" I asked. I was trying to think of a reason to get him to look in my direction, but none came to mind.

"I guess," he said, still preoccupied with his car.

"You hungry?" I asked, putting down the hose.

"Not really," he said, backing out of the car.

Before I could pick up the hose, he doused me with a Super Soaker water gun.

I reached for the hose, but there was so much water in my eyes I couldn't see, and my brother just kept assaulting me.

By the time I got him back, I was soaking wet.

We were laughing so hard we could barely breathe when Mama and Daddy pulled up in the driveway.

"What a great sight," Daddy said, grinning as he got out of the car. "Hey, baby." He walked over and gave me a kiss.

"Hey, Daddy," I said, hugging him despite my wet clothes.

I looked beyond him at Mama and gave her a tight smile. "Hi," I said.

"Hi, Jasmine," she said. "It's good to see you."

"You, too," I said, looking at her. She looked older, and I realized I really had missed her.

"Would you like to go out to dinner with us?" she asked. "We're going to celebrate my promotion."

"You got a promotion?" I asked. It felt weird not to know what was going on in her life.

She nodded and smiled.

"Congratulations, Mama," I said. Part of me wanted to go and hug her, but I ignored the urge.

"Thanks, baby," she said. She walked over and wrapped her arms around me and squeezed me tight. "It's good to see you, Jasmine. So good."

I held myself stiff for a few seconds; then, before I knew it, I had melted into her arms and was crying every tear that was in me.

It was good feeling as though I was part of a real family again. For weeks I had been trying to pretend that T and Loretta were my family, but truthfully, I really did miss Mama and Daddy.

We went to Red Lobster and had a good time just laughing and talking—being a family.

Once we'd finished eating, we headed back to the house, and I hung out for a little while, then got up to leave.

"Where are you going?" Mama asked.

"Back to Loretta's," I said, looking for my keys in my purse.

"Baby, you don't have to do that," Daddy said. "Your room's still waiting for you."

"You're welcome to stay," Mama said.

I got excited at the thought.

"Know that living here means you're going to live by my rules," she said.

I remembered what T had said to me about making up with Mama, then thought about her rules, which were part of the reason I had left in the first place. In a few short weeks, I had gotten a taste of freedom, and I wasn't trying to go back. I still hadn't told Mama and Daddy about not going to college, but I guessed they assumed that that hadn't changed.

I looked at Derrick, and he nodded at me, silently asking me to stay, but I wasn't feeling it. "I'll come back and visit soon," I said quietly as I grasped my keys.

Mama just gave me a sad smile before she walked over to me. "No matter what you think, our door is always open to you. I love you, and I miss you," she said. She looked back at Derrick. "We all do."

I didn't know what to say, so I just turned and walked out the door.

I thought about going back home the entire week leading up to the competition. I talked about it with T a couple of times, and as usual he encouraged me to make up with Mama and go back home, but I still wasn't feeling it. We had visited a few more houses, but none of them felt like home to me, so I passed on the chance to buy them.

The night before the competition I spent the night at T's house. I had never done that before, but it felt good to wake up in his arms. I was starting to think more and more about having sex with him, but every time the thought came to me, Kyle crossed my mind.

The morning of the competition, T presented me with breakfast in bed. As he fed me a strawberry, I couldn't help but smile. I reminded myself to remember every detail about the day, because once I won my record deal, it was going to be the day that changed my life.

"You nervous?" T asked.

"Of course not," I said. "I never get nervous before a performance."

"Are you and your brother going to practice today?"

"Only for a little while," I said. "I hate that we didn't get to practice more, but we've been so busy."

"You guys will be great," he said, giving me a kiss.

"You're still coming, right?" I asked.

"I'll be in the front row," he said.

T and I hung out for a few more hours before I headed to pick up Derrick.

"We're going to have to take your car," he said the moment he let me in the house. I still had my key, but I felt funny just walking in.

"What's wrong with your clunker?" I asked.

"I think it needs a new battery," he said.

"Why don't you just buy a new car?" I said.

"Because I like the one I have. Besides, everyone doesn't have a savings account like yours, Little Miss Moneybags," he joked.

"You know I'll give you the money," I said seriously.

"I know you will," he said.

Derrick went to finish getting dressed. "Let's do it," he said when he returned.

I turned to walk out the door. "Where are Mama and Daddy?" I asked when it finally occurred to me that the house was really quiet.

"They had some errands to run," he said, "but they said they'd be at the competition."

I looked at him in amazement. "Mama and Daddy are actually coming to see us perform?"

He grinned and nodded. "Yeah, I was shocked when they told me, too."

We headed to the Apollo Theater in Harlem, and

after signing in, we ran through our routine one more time. It still amazed me how well me and my brother vibed when we were onstage.

We went and grabbed a bite to eat after we finished; then we headed backstage to get dressed. I had bought us coordinating Rocawear outfits. We were going on last again.

I was sitting there chilling when I smelled cigar smoke. I looked up and smiled.

"Don't you see the no-smoking sign in here?" I teased.

DC laughed at me. He had on a pink suit with a white shirt and pink tie, as well as a pink hat and pink shoes. I'd always thought men looked funny in pink, but the outfit didn't look too bad on him.

"Miss Jasmine, how are you?" he asked, extending his arm for me to give him a hug.

"Hey, DC," I said. "I didn't think you'd be here."

He stuck his cigar in his mouth and spoke around it. "We've got to check out the competition," he said, turning to the man behind him. "Right, Ron?"

"Oh, hey, Ron. I didn't even see you," I said, giving him a hug, as well.

He just nodded at me before disappearing somewhere.

DC looked around to see if anyone was near us. "You know my offer still stands about giving you a record deal," he said.

"Thanks, DC," I said.

"I see you're up to your old tricks," a deep voice said.

"Kevin, what's up?" DC said, giving the guy a brother-man handshake. "Jasmine, this is Kevin Mitchell, my protégé and the owner of Image Records."

"It's nice to meet you, Kevin," I said. "I guess we'll be working together pretty soon. I've already got some great ideas for my album. My boyfriend is going to be the producer."

He laughed. "I love your enthusiasm," he said. "Good luck tonight."

"I don't need luck, but thanks anyway," I said before he walked away.

DC looked at me once again. "Remember, the door is always open at DC Records," he said.

I nodded and gave him another hug before he left.

I looked around for Derrick but I didn't see him anywhere, so I peeped behind the curtain and looked into the audience. The place was packed. It was only a few minutes before showtime, and as promised, T was sitting in the front row. DC went and sat right next to him, and they began talking like they knew each other.

I spotted Loretta and Kyle, and I tried to ignore how my heart sped up at the sight of Kyle. As though he could feel me staring, he glanced up and our eyes locked. I looked away, pretending I hadn't seen him, then searched for my brother and my parents, but with all the people I couldn't find them.

My gaze landed on T again, and he looked up and blew me a kiss, which I returned. He looked like he was about to get up and come backstage, but before he could, Robby Rob, an up-and-coming comedian who was emceeing the event, started the show.

"Good evening, and welcome to our first annual All-City Invitational. Before the night is over, someone will walk away with a record deal, y'all."

The audience started applauding, and the reality of the evening hit me.

"You okay?" Derrick asked, coming from out of nowhere.

"Where've you been?" I asked, ignoring his question.

"Out front hanging with Kyle and Loretta," he said.

I didn't get a chance to respond before the first group brushed past us to get onstage.

They were decent, as were the three acts that followed, but they had nothing on us.

When it was time for Derrick and me to hit the stage, my adrenaline kicked in, and as always, I let the music take control. I played harder than I had ever played before, and Derrick was rocking it so hard the entire audience was on its feet.

As rehearsed, Derrick made his way behind the turntable when I took center stage, and I lost myself in the music. I freestyled a rap; then I let loose with some Mary J. Blige–style singing that had grown men slapping five. I caught a brief glimpse of Mama and Daddy, and Mama was standing there with her mouth wide open in amazement.

Once I was done, I made my way back behind my turntable and scratched out one final beat, which signaled the end of our performance. As always, when we finished, I came from behind the table, Derrick and I grabbed hands and we took a bow before running off stage.

"Man, we killed it," I said, giving Derrick a high five.

He nodded as sweat poured off him. I handed him a towel; then we waited for the results to be announced.

I saw Kevin of Image Records waiting backstage

across the room, and he when gave me a slight nod, I knew we were in.

Finally, thirty minutes after our performance, all five groups were called back to the stage, and the third-place winner was called. I really tuned Kevin out, wishing he would call our name for the record deal.

It wasn't until a chorus of boos echoed around the room and I felt Derrick tugging my hand that I realized something was wrong.

"Come on," he mouthed.

He led me to the stage, where we were handed a trophy and a check for five thousand dollars, but reality didn't set in until the first-place winner, the group from Staten Island, was called.

I just stared in amazement, knowing this had to be a nightmare. There was no way we had lost to such a wack group. Their performance couldn't compare to ours on any level.

I managed to get to the car before I broke down. Derrick started the car, and of all songs, the one I had recorded with Mocha Love blasted through the speakers. I snapped off the radio and cried even harder.

We were halfway home before Derrick spoke.

"I'm sorry, Jas. I know how much this meant to you," he said.

I didn't say anything for a second, not really knowing what to say.

"It just wasn't meant to be," he said. "Maybe this is your sign that you should really be going to college."

I turned and glared at him. "You did this on purpose," I said. "You didn't want a record deal, and you didn't want me to have one, either."

"Come on, Jas. You know that's not true."

"You make me sick," I screamed. "Did Mama put you up to this?"

He took his eyes off the road long enough to stare at me in amazement. "What would make you think we would mess this up for you?" he asked.

"I know how much Mama hates my music, and all you care about is going to college. You did this on purpose. You didn't do anything we practiced. Now that I think about it, you've been avoiding practicing all summer."

"You know that's not—"

"Shut up. Just shut up," I screamed. "You make me sick. I hate you!" My heart was beating so fast that I felt it in my ears, and I know my face had to be almost red with anger. I hadn't been that upset in a long time.

We had made it to Queens, and we stopped at a

traffic light. I jumped out of the car, not even wanting to be in the same space as my brother.

"Jasmine, get back in here," Derrick yelled, but I ignored him. "Jasmine, get in this car—now!"

"Leave me alone," I said. I walked, not really sure where I was going.

I heard Derrick park the car, but I ignored him. When he came up behind me and grabbed my arm, I snatched it away.

"Jas, I'm sorry you lost," he said, reaching for me again.

"No, you're not," I said. "The only reason you performed is because I begged you to. You didn't want the record deal anyway."

I tried to stop the tears from sliding down my cheeks, but they still came. I just stood there in silence for a while, stunned that I had lost. I had never lost anything in my life, and it hurt.

Derrick gave me a hug. "You know I've always had your back," he said softly. "I'm sorry you lost, but it's not over. You're still going to get your record deal."

He led me back to the car, and I took a deep breath, trying to get myself together to figure out my next move.

* * *

When I woke up the next morning, it took me a second to realize I was in my old bedroom. I didn't even remember falling asleep.

It was only eight in the morning, and although I had been asleep for almost eight hours, it felt like I hadn't gotten any rest. I wanted to believe the night before was just a bad dream, but the way I was feeling told me it wasn't.

I finally got out of bed two hours later. It was Sunday, and I assumed that everyone had gone to church, but when I walked into the kitchen, Mama was sitting at the table sipping a cup of coffee.

When she saw me, she walked over to me and just wrapped me in her arms. "You did a great job last night. I'm sorry you didn't win," she said.

Her words made me angry all over again. "No, you're not," I said. "You've never wanted me to have a deal, either. You hate my music. That's part of the reason I moved out."

Mama looked at me, and I noticed a sadness in her eyes. "Baby, I don't hate your music," she said, leading me to the table. After I was seated, she busied herself making pancakes.

We sat in silence for a while, and just when I decided that I was going to head back to Loretta's house, she spoke. "You know, your daddy loved his music, and I was really happy for him when he, your uncle and Chubby landed their record deal."

"You were?" I asked skeptically.

She nodded and smiled as though she was thinking about the past. "We spent so many nights in the recording studio that it didn't make sense, and I was at every gig."

"You were?" I asked.

She nodded and took a seat across from me. "I was your daddy's biggest fan. When I found out I was pregnant, I wanted him to go ahead and pursue his music, but his mother talked him into letting it go—said he needed something more stable for his family. He was depressed for a long time, and I tried to talk him into going back to his music, but he didn't. I didn't understand why until years later, when I found out that Chubby had talked them into some crazy deal, and if they didn't deliver the people were going to kill your father and uncle. I thought your father was working overtime at his job, but really he was recording—songs he never saw one cent of the money for. It took him years to pay off those debts, but even still, he loved the music. Seeing him work so hard with nothing to show for it made me angry. I got to the point where just seeing an instrument made me sick to my stomach. When he finally made good on the contract, he put away his instruments for a few years, and we had a good life—until that day you found that turntable."

She gave a brief laugh and shook her head. "I saw that spark in your eye even then. I've always tried to discourage you, because I know how shady this business can be. I figured if I wasn't involved or didn't show my support you would eventually lose interest. I didn't want you to be hurt.

"I'm sorry you lost the competition, baby, but part of me is glad that you did. I hope this will make you reconsider going to school. You guys aren't supposed to go until next week, so you still have time."

I looked at her in surprise, and she laughed. "You had to know that I realized a long time ago that you really weren't planning on going to school."

I found myself laughing, too. I had been trying to hide the truth from her, but the real truth was that my mother knew me better than anyone.

She got up and finished fixing the pancakes, then placed a big plate of them in front of me before serving herself.

"Where are Daddy and Derrick?" I asked.

"I don't know," she said. "They were both gone when I got up this morning."

We ate in silence for a few more minutes.

"So how has it been living on your own?"

"Good," I said.

"I used to always dream of packing up my bags and leaving, but I never had the nerve to do it. I've always admired that about you, Jasmine. You've got a lot of spunk. Never lose that."

I nodded.

"So you ready to come back home yet?"

I thought about her question. I really did enjoy being able to come and go as I pleased, but there was nothing like knowing I had somewhere I could really call home to lay my head every night. The more I thought about it, the more I realized that I did miss being at home.

"Yeah, I'm ready to come back," I said softly, looking at the floor.

"This door is always open to you," she said, and smiled.

I smiled, too, realizing that T would be happy that I'd finally made things right with Mama.

"So tell me about this boy you've been seeing," she said, as though reading my mind.

I looked at her in surprise.

"Now, you couldn't possibly think that I haven't been keeping up with what's going on in your life," she said.

"But who told you?" I said, highly doubting it was my brother.

"Kyle called here complaining about you seeing this grown man."

I groaned. "He has been driving me crazy," I said, our kiss flashing through my mind. I quickly erased the thought.

"He's in love with you," Mama said matter-of-factly.

"You think so?" I asked, and my heart sped up in a way it never did when I thought about T.

"Of course. That boy has been in love with you for years, and although you probably won't admit it to yourself, you're in love with him, too."

I didn't know how to respond to that, so I drank some milk.

"So this T fellow is almost twenty?"

I nodded.

"You know, Jas, that's really too old for you," she began, but then she looked at me. "But I'm going to let you make your own decision."

"Thanks, Mama," I said, getting up to give her a hug.

"So when are you moving back?" she asked.

"Why not today?" I said.

"Sounds good."

After breakfast, I went to get my keys so I could go get my stuff from Loretta's. I finally found them in my purse. As I was grabbing my purse, my phone vibrated, indicating I had a message—actually, a few of them. T had called a few times, sounding worried as had Loretta and Kyle. I decided I'd swing by T's house, then head to Loretta's. I'd figure out what to do about Kyle on the way.

When I let myself into T's house, the place was dark, so I figured he was out. I was trying to find a piece of paper and a pen to leave him a note when I heard voices coming from his recording studio.

I smiled, realizing that T was home, and I was suddenly excited to see him.

I threw the door open, and it took a second for the pungent odor of marijuana to hit me.

At the same time, I caught sight of T and Loretta tangled on the sofa. They were so into what they were doing that they didn't notice me—until I walked up and slapped the fool out of Loretta, whose big breasts were swinging all in T's face.

She was so into the kiss that it took a while for her to react. When she finally opened her desire-filled eyes and looked at me, her eyes widened in shock. By then, T was pushing her off him.

I was so angry I couldn't speak. I turned to walk out of the room, but then the image of what I had seen five minutes before flashed before my eyes. I swung back around and hauled off and punched Loretta in her face again. T tried to step between us, and I swung on him, too.

"Y'all can have each other," I screamed. "I can't believe this."

As much as I wanted to collapse on the floor, I didn't want to give them the privilege of seeing me that way. With all the dignity I could muster, I removed T's heart-shaped key chain from my key ring and handed it to him. "Looks like your heart really doesn't belong to me," I said quietly.

"Baby, don't do this," he said. "I'm so sorry."

I didn't even bother to respond.

I headed out to my car and drove to Loretta's, determined to have all my stuff moved out before she got there.

I went in to find her mother lying across the sofa, drunk. I just shook my head and started gathering my things. It took me two trips to my house, but I finally moved everything—and I realized if I had left anything behind, it wasn't worth having.

After deciding I'd unload my car later, I headed to

my room. I met Mama coming out of the bathroom. She must have seen the pain on my face because she grabbed me and didn't let go, and that was when the tears came. She didn't say a word. She just rocked me for what seemed like hours. When I felt as though I couldn't cry anymore, she tucked me into bed, pulled the covers up to my chin and kissed my forehead.

I didn't think I would be able to sleep, but the past few days had finally caught up with me. When I woke up, the sun was shining.

I went to the bathroom, then headed to the kitchen, where my brother was sitting at the table.

"Girl, I was just about to come check on you."

"I'm okay," I said. "I was just a little tired."

"I guess so. You've been asleep since yesterday morning."

I looked at him like he was crazy. "What?" I finally managed to say.

"Yeah," he said. He looked at me. "You okay?"

The image of T and Loretta together flashed through my mind. "I'll be fine," I said quietly.

He just nodded. "Welcome home," he finally said.

I smiled, liking the sound of that.

"What do you have planned today?" I asked.

"I'm going to try and finish packing."

It took me a while to remember what he was

talking about. "Oh, yeah. I forgot school starts next week. When are you leaving?"

"Friday," he said.

I looked at him curiously, and he read my question on my face.

"I have the symposium this weekend."

I nodded.

"You know, Jas, it's not too late for you to go to school with me."

I thought about what he said. "I know," I finally said, "but that's not what I want to do."

"So what are you going to do?" he asked. He got up to grab a bowl of cereal, holding up his bowl to silently ask if I wanted some, too. I nodded.

"I don't know yet. I guess I figured I would be cutting my album." I thought about all the money I had been saving. "Maybe I can do it myself," I said.

"You can do that while you go to school," he said, passing me a bowl of Froot Loops and some milk.

"Yeah, I could," I said thoughtfully, "but to get things jumping I need to stay in New York."

"Well, I guess I can come home a couple of weekends and make a guest appearance on the album," he said.

"Thank you," I said, getting up to give him a hug.

"For what?" he asked.

"For being my big brother," I said.

"Girl, go somewhere with that mess," he said, pushing me away, but I saw him smiling.

I headed back to my room to get dressed. I had just gotten out of the shower when my cell phone rang. I figured it was probably T or Loretta, so I decided to let it go to voice mail.

I figured I would have a whole bunch of e-mails from both T and Loretta apologizing. There were only three messages—one from Kyle, another from the guy who had paid me to DJ his party and another from Jessica, DC's assistant.

Jessica sounded busy as usual when I called, but she brightened up when she heard my voice. "Hey, Jasmine," she said. "DC told me to put you right through. Hang on." She put me on hold, and I listened to one of the latest top ten hits by one of DC Records' artists before DC came on the line.

"Good morning," he said, and I wondered if he had a cigar in his mouth.

"Good morning," I said.

"So, you ready to get started on your album?"

"What are you talking about?" I asked.

He laughed. "Oh, you get so many offers to record an album that you've forgotten all about mine?"

"You were serious about that?" I said.

He laughed again. "Look, I don't have time to play games," he said. "I'm serious about changing my company's image, and I think you're just the person to do it."

I grinned, realizing my dreams of landing a record deal were going to come true despite losing All-City.

"Cool," I said.

"So when can you guys come in so we can negotiate this deal?"

"You guys?" I said.

"You and your brother. Word is you guys are a package deal."

"Oh, you don't have to worry about him," I said.

"I've heard him. He needs to be on the album," DC said.

I knew Derrick didn't really like DC, but he had just offered to be on my album if I did it myself, so I didn't think he would mind.

"When do you want us there?" I asked.

"Tomorrow morning," he said.

We wrapped up the details for the next day; then I went to find my brother, who was in his room packing. He must have felt my presence, because he looked up. "What?" he said.

"I got a record deal."

His mouth dropped open. "Are you serious?" he said.

"DC just offered it to me," I said.

He rolled his eyes and turned away. "I know you're not going to record with that man," he said, his back to me.

"Derrick, come on. He's trying to change the image of the label."

"But that's not going to change his image. The man is slime, Jas. You know that. Just stick with your plan of doing the album yourself. Your boyfriend and Kyle can help you with it."

His mention of T brought tears to my eyes, but I refused to focus on him. "Why should I spend my own money for an album when DC's willing to spend his? Besides, he wants you on the album, too. With the money you'll make, you can pay for school."

"I am not going to be on your album if you sign with DC."

"Derrick, why are you tripping?" I asked.

"No, Jas, why are you tripping?"

"Fine," I said. I realized there was no point in arguing with him, although I had already decided I was going to convince him to be on the album.

I spent the rest of the day waiting to hear from T

or Loretta. T finally called, but I didn't want to speak to him. It was enough for me to know that he at least felt a little sorry for what had happened.

When Mama and Daddy got home, we decided to go out to dinner to celebrate everyone being home.

"I'm going to enjoy this moment while I can," Mama said as we were walking out the door. "Both my babies will be gone next week."

I guess she thought everything was really back to normal, but I had to quickly set her straight.

"Mama," I said, "I'm still not going to school."

I saw the anger in her eyes, but before she could say anything, Daddy touched her hand, silently asking her to be quiet.

"Let's talk about this later," he said. "It's been a little while since we've gone out together as a family, and I want to enjoy it."

Everyone agreed, although there was a tense quietness all the way to the restaurant.

After we ordered, I decided to bring up me not going to college. I figured there wasn't much yelling Mama would do in a restaurant.

I was wrong.

After I told Mama and Daddy about my deal with DC Records, Mama really lost it.

"You will not be signing with that man," she said.

She glared at me, daring me to say something, and I looked back at her just as hard.

"Yes, I will be," I said. "He's offering me a chance at my dream, and I'm not going to let you or anyone else stop me."

"Little girl, you forget that you're living under my roof—"

"But that can change," I said. "I moved out before, and I can do it again."

People were starting to look at us, but I didn't care.

"Why don't we finish this conversation at home?" Daddy said quietly.

"Don't bother," I said. I pushed back my chair.

"Don't you move," Daddy said. It was very rare that he got angry with me, but when he did, I knew not to cross him. This was one of those times. "I'm not going to put up with you running away again. We are going to work through this as a family. Now, we're going to sit here and finish our dinner like we have some sense. Derrick, pass me the salt."

Derrick and I both did as we were told.

Somehow we made it through dinner. Daddy tried to make polite conversation, but it didn't work. When we finally got home, I expected Mama to go off.

Instead, she looked at me and shook her head.

"You know what? Do what you want to do. I'm tired. I'm done. If you want to ruin your life, I'm not going to stop you."

"Baby, don't say that," Daddy said.

"No, Daddy, it's okay. We all know how Mama really feels. She doesn't like me doing the music. I get it. It's cool. I won't sign with DC Records," I said.

I turned around and walked to my room, not really caring anymore. In a few short days, I had lost not one but two record deals. There was no way life could get any worse.

chapter 10

I was awake most of the night thinking about the last few days. It was around daybreak when I decided that I was not going to let Mama kill my dream. DC was offering me the opportunity of a lifetime, and I was going to take it.

I was up by seven so I could make into the city for my eleven o'clock meeting with DC.

I had just sat down to eat a bowl of cereal when Derrick walked into the kitchen. "What are you doing up so early?" he asked.

I had decided I wasn't going to tell anyone about accepting the record deal until after the contracts were signed, so I said, "I'm going to check out NYU. Maybe I'll go to school there."

"For real?" he said, looking excited. "You want me to go with you?"

"Nah, it's okay," I said quickly. I had never lied to my brother, and I knew he was going to see straight through it, but he didn't.

"No, I'll go with you," he insisted. "I see Mama finally got to you."

I just smiled. I thought about leaving without my brother while he was getting dressed, but I decided not to. Even if he didn't agree with what I was doing, I knew he'd have my back. I was running late, so Derrick said he'd drive me.

Derrick looked at me crazy when I told him to park on the same block as DC Records, but he didn't say a word. As we approached the office, he stopped me.

"What are you doing?" he asked.

"What does it look like?" I said.

"Jas, you are not signing with these people."

"Watch me," I said, pulling open the glass door so I could head into the building.

"I can't let you do this."

"Look, I've made up my mind that I'm signing with DC, so if you have a problem with that, you need to go wait in the car."

He must have seen the determination on my face, because he just sighed and followed me inside.

* * *

I wasn't sure what kind of office to expect, but what greeted me was actually very nice. After being ushered past the receptionist's desk, I made it to DC's inner office, which had comfortable leather furniture, as well as copies of what looked like hundreds of gold records.

I spotted Jessica immediately, although she hadn't said a word. She looked like I had pictured her—a younger version of Halle Berry.

She seemed stressed, kind of the way she always sounded, but her face brightened when she saw me.

"Hey, Jasmine," she said as though we saw each other every day. It was kind of hard to believe it was our first time meeting.

"Hi, Jessica," I said. I turned to Derrick. "This is my brother."

"Nice to meet you," Jessica said.

Derrick just nodded.

"So today's the big day, huh?" she said, turning to me.

"Yeah. It looks that way," I said.

We all looked up when the door behind Jessica opened and DC walked out. He was wearing a red suit with a black shirt and a red tie along with a red hat.

"Hey, Jasmine," he said, sticking his trademark cigar in his mouth, then extending his arms for a hug.

I hugged him then turned to Derrick. "Do you remember my brother?" I said.

"Derrick, nice seeing you again." DC extended his hand.

I could tell Derrick didn't want to speak, but he knew better than to be disrespectful. "How are you?" he said.

"You guys come on in." DC led us into the biggest office I had ever seen. It looked bigger than our whole house.

Derrick and I settled into two chairs in front of DC's desk and waited while he shuffled through some papers. He was just about to speak when a knock sounded on the door. Before DC could respond, the door swung open and in walked his partner, Ron.

"Hey, guys," he said, shaking Derrick's hand, then leaning over to give me a hug.

"Hi," I said, excited. For some reason, his presence made the record deal more real to me.

"Let's get down to business," DC said after Ron was seated.

I sat up straight, trying to look as professional as

possible, while Derrick slumped in his seat, looking bored. I gave him the eye, but he ignored me.

"Jasmine, we really believe you have a future with this company. We are committed to taking you all the way to the top. As you know, we've had some trouble with some of our artists in the past, but we want to change our image, and we believe you are the person to help us do that. I know the best producers in the business, and I know we're going to produce a chart-topping album.

"I've taken the liberty of drawing up a contract for you. It's our standard new-artist agreement. We believe in you so much, we want to sign you for five albums." DC slid the contract and a pen toward me, and as I started to sign my name, Derrick grabbed my arm.

"You need to have Uncle Henry look that over," he said.

I ignored him. What was my uncle going to do? DC had said it was the standard new-artist contract, so it wasn't like I could make changes to it. Plus, if I told my uncle, he would tell my parents, and I didn't want them to know anything about my deal until the contract was signed.

I finished signing my name and slid the contract back to DC, who grinned and stuck out his hand. "Welcome to DC Records," he said before he began talking about recording, going on tour and promoting my album.

I heard everything he was saying, but at the same time, I was daydreaming about taking center stage before a crowd screaming my name as I stood in the spotlight.

"Triple T has already agreed to produce a few of your songs," I heard Ron say.

"What?" I asked, quickly focusing on the conversation.

"I spoke with him this morning, and he said you guys have already spoken and that he even has a few songs you recorded together."

"I don't want him on my album," I said sharply.

Ron ignored me and turned to Derrick. "We also want you to rap on a few of the singles. Of course, you'll be compensated."

Derrick laughed under his breath. "Thanks but no thanks," he said. He got up from the chair and walked toward the door. "I'm going to wait downstairs."

I was so embarrassed. "Derrick, what are you doing?" I asked, running over to him.

"You didn't need to sign with these clowns, Jas." He didn't seem to care if they heard him or not. I looked back, and it was pretty obvious they had heard him.

"Excuse us," I said; then I led Derrick into a small

conference room Jessica said we could use. "What are you doing?"

"No, what are you doing?" Derrick yelled. "You just sold your soul to the devil. Why would you sign a deal for five records? You're going to be recording with them forever."

I thought about what my brother was saying and realized he was right. Five albums sounded good, but if I only put out something every two years, that meant I could be working for DC Records for the next ten years. I knew they were trying to change their image, but they hadn't done it yet. Plus, they had already hooked me up with Triple T, and I knew I never wanted to see him again after what went down with him and Loretta, but judging by the way Ron had ignored my objections, I really didn't have a choice. I decided not to worry about all that.

"Why are you messing this up for me?" I said, putting aside my doubts.

"You're messing this up for yourself," Derrick said. He took a deep breath, then shook his head at me. "I'm going to wait downstairs while you finish up."

DC and Ron went over a few more things before they handed me a copy of the contract. I went downstairs to find Derrick sitting in the car listening to the radio. He smiled when he saw me, which I took as a good sign that he wasn't mad.

"I got my deal. You're looking at DC Records' newest artist," I said, waving my contract at him.

He took it from me and gave me a sad smile.

"You're not going to congratulate me?" I said.

"Congratulations," he said, but I could tell he didn't mean it.

His attitude made me mad all over again. "You know what? Forget you. You're just jealous because I'm already living my dream," I said. "I didn't have to set foot in college, and I'm already making more money than you."

"Whatever, Jas," he said. He went to start his car, but it just sputtered. He tried it several times, but the same thing kept happening.

"It sounds like the battery's dead again," he said. He got out of the car and went to check under the hood. I slid down in my seat, embarrassed. I was about to become a household name and I was sitting in my brother's broke-down car.

"Start it again," he said.

"You need to get another car," I mumbled as I leaned over and started the ignition.

He stuck his head in the driver's-side window. "Everybody doesn't have money like you, Jas."

"I'll buy you a car," I said.

"What do I look like, letting my little sister buy me a car?" he said. "I can afford to buy my own car."

"Doesn't look like it," I said, rolling my eyes.

Derrick snatched open the door. "You know what? I'm about sick of you. You're starting to act just like these people at DC records. You're turning into a money-hungry little witch."

He looked as surprised at having said the words as I felt at having heard them. My mouth dropped open.

"I'm sorry," he said.

I just shook my head. "No, you're not."

When he didn't respond, it just made me feel worse. We sat there in silence for a few minutes, until I finally couldn't take it anymore.

"So you're not going to apologize?" I asked.

He slowly shook his head. "Not for telling the truth," he said.

I nodded and reached for the door handle. "Forget you, Derrick. You make me sick. I hate you." I slammed the door and started walking toward the subway.

"Where are you going?" he asked.

I didn't even bother to respond. Tears fell, and I wiped them away. I'd thought that if anyone would always understand me, it would be my brother. On what was supposed to be the happiest day of my life, I felt as though my world was crashing down around me.

I was about a block away when I heard what sounded like a car engine backfiring. It really didn't register until it happened three more times that it was gunshots. I instinctively ducked, just like the other people on the sidewalk, and once the shots were over, I thought of my brother.

I found myself running down the block, where a crowd was forming. I searched it for my brother, but I didn't see him.

"Derrick—" I yelled, but he didn't answer me, so I yelled a little louder, but he didn't say anything.

People were starting to look at me, but I didn't care. I knew my brother had to be nearby because his car was still parked, so I tore through the crowd screaming his name.

That was when I saw him.

It took a few seconds for it to hit me that he was on the ground. He looked like he had just fallen and hadn't yet managed to get up. I hurried over to give him a hand.

That was when I saw the blood.

It was everywhere, spurting out of his chest like a fountain.

"Derrick," I whispered, not believing what I was seeing.

He tried to talk, but blood came out of his mouth, too.

I slid down beside him and grabbed his head. "Don't talk," I said. I blindly looked into the crowd. "Can someone call 911?"

I didn't even wait for an answer as I refocused on my brother.

"You're going to be okay. Help is coming," I said, looking into his eyes.

He looked so scared, and I remembered the time when we were little and I fell out of a tree and broke my arm in two places. Derrick had sat beside me like I was doing now for him, and I was sure I had the same look of fear in my eyes he'd had in his all those years ago.

I just sat holding and rocking him trying to offer words of comfort until I heard the sirens. The ambulance and police pulled up about the same time, and the emergency medical technicians pretty much had to rip my brother from my arms so they could work on him.

When they finally got him stable enough, they put him in the ambulance, and I jumped in right behind them, praying like I had never prayed before.

My brother died on the way to the hospital.

I sat and watched helplessly as the EMTs worked on him, trying to save his life, but in the end, he just slipped away.

I didn't remember much after that. Someone called my parents, and they came to the hospital looking as shocked as I felt. Actually, I was more numb than anything. My brother was my everything—my best friend, my world. There was no way he was gone.

When we finally made it back to the house later that evening, I kept waiting on him to walk through the door. When that didn't happen, I told myself he was out hanging with Kyle or at work, and that I would see him soon.

I slept with my parents that night, still trying to make sense of what happened.

When I woke up the next morning, I was in their bed alone. I sat up laughing at the bad dream I'd had, and I got up to go tell my brother, knowing he was going to tell me how silly I was for letting a dream spook me.

The joke was on me.

When I walked into the living room, it was filled with people, food and flowers. I knew then that I hadn't been dreaming. I had witnessed a similar scene when my grandmother died a few years ago, but this one was different because most of the people sitting in the room were kids.

Kyle was the first one to spot me, and without saying a word, he just walked over and grabbed me. That was when I lost it. From the depths of my soul, tears erupted, and I cried for what seemed like days. I vaguely remembered Daddy lifting me up and carrying me to my room. A few minutes later, darkness claimed me.

When I woke again, it was dark outside, but I could make out Kyle sitting in a chair. I stared at him for a few seconds. He must have sensed I was awake, because he walked over to the bed and grabbed my hand and squeezed it like he would never let go.

"We're going to get through this, Jas," he vowed.

I just nodded.

He sat down beside me, and we sat in silence for a few minutes.

"Are all those people still here?" I asked.

He shook his head. "Most of them have already left. I think Loretta and T are here, and a few of your relatives."

I struggled to sit up. "What are they doing here?" I asked, angry that either of them would have the nerve to set foot in my house.

"I guess they wanted to offer their condolences."

"Tell them to leave," I said. "I don't want to see either one of them." My tone must have told him I meant business, because he didn't ask any questions—he just went to do as I had asked.

I rolled over on my back and stared at the ceiling after he left, still hoping I was just dreaming. When I heard the door creak open, I didn't have the energy to see who it was.

"Jas, you asleep?" someone asked.

I turned at the sound of the voice and smiled when I saw Kyle's little brother, Tony.

He walked over to the bed and climbed up beside me. "Hi," he said when he realized I was awake. He gave me the biggest smile, and I couldn't help but smile, too, although it didn't last long.

"Hey, Tony," I said.

He snuggled up beside me. "I'm sorry about Derrick," he said into the darkness.

"Thank you," I said quietly.

I realized that I would be hearing "I'm sorry" a lot over the next few days. "Thank you" felt like a silly response, but I didn't know what else to say.

"You want me to get you something to eat?" he asked.

I realized that I was hungry, and I thought about asking him to fix me a plate, but I could only imagine what Tony would put on it. Instead, I got up and headed to the living room, where my family and Kyle's mother were sitting.

I was glad to see that T and Loretta were nowhere around.

Mama walked over to me and gave me a hug. "You hungry?" she asked.

I nodded, and she went to fix me a plate.

My butt had just hit the chair when Uncle Henry started in.

"So what happened?" he asked me.

"Henry," someone said, shocked at how forward he was being.

He ignored them and stared at me, waiting for a response.

"I don't know," I finally said. "I was a block away when I heard gunshots."

"So you didn't see anything?" he asked, sounding as though he didn't believe me.

"No," I said.

"Why were you near DC Records?" he asked.

"Why is that any of your business?" I returned.

He looked like I had slapped him.

"I'm trying to help you," he said.

"Unless you can bring my brother back, don't bother." I pushed aside the plate of food Mama had brought me and headed back to my room, not wanting to deal with my family. I crawled into bed and seriously thought about never leaving. When I heard the door creak open again, I pretended to be asleep. I opened my eyes when I felt someone sit beside me and take my hand. Kyle had once again taken up his post, and I smiled my thanks, knowing that, like my brother, he had my back.

chapter 11

The day of my brother's funeral was the hardest of my life. I had refused to go to view the body, because I still didn't want to believe my brother was gone. I just kept telling myself that he was at the symposium he was supposed to attend that weekend.

His murder had been all over the news for the last couple of days, Kyle had told me. There was still no clue as to the killer. After searching his car, the police had allowed Daddy to pick it up, and he had just parked it in the garage. I found myself going to sit in it a couple of times because it made me feel closer to my brother.

Back in my room I took a deep breath as I looked at myself in the mirror, silently encouraging myself to get it together. When a soft knock sounded at the door, I couldn't even respond before the door was pushed open and in walked Loretta.

I just stared at her in amazement. First off, I couldn't believe she had the nerve to show up at my house, especially on the day of my brother's funeral. Second, she looked a mess. She had on a black satin shirtdress that stopped right below her butt and left her breasts spilling out, some fishnet stockings and wedge-heeled sandals. If that wasn't bad enough, she had on this blue pageboy wig.

"Hey," she said softly. Her eyes were red, I assumed from crying, but I realized it could have been from any number of things. Loretta had been my girl for a long time, but I realized in that moment that I'd never really known her.

I didn't bother to respond. Instead, I turned around and played with my hair, which as usual wasn't cooperating.

"Look, I know you're mad at me, and I just wanted to say I'm sorry…for everything."

I applied my lip gloss and puckered my lips in the mirror, still ignoring her.

"T knows some people who knows some people out in L.A. who can help me get some modeling gigs," she said. "I'm leaving tomorrow."

I laughed to myself. I couldn't believe she had the nerve to mention T. I just shook my head.

"Aren't you going to say anything?" she asked.

"Bye," I said into the mirror, looking her dead in the eye.

"Why are you tripping?" she said. "T didn't mean anything to me. I just did what I had to do for my career."

"Don't you mean you did who you had to do?" I asked, walking over to the bed, where I put on my shoes. My parents and I had agreed not to wear black, so I'd chosen a red pantsuit and some black heels.

"Trust me. You'll thank me later. T wasn't who you thought he was."

"And neither were you," I said.

She gave me a sad nod. "I guess I deserve that."

I finally looked at her. "Why are you here?" I asked.

"Because you're my friend, and I loved Derrick like a brother," she said, shaking her head in amazement. "I still can't believe he's gone. I'm so sorry."

"Yeah, you are sorry," I said. "Please leave me alone." I brushed past her and headed to the living room, where my parents and few other family members were gathered along with Kyle and his family.

I didn't even acknowledge Loretta when she walked out the door. Kyle looked at me, silently asking if I was all right, and I nodded. If I never saw Loretta again, it would be too soon.

We said a brief prayer, then headed to the church, which was packed. I stood between my parents in the processional line, trying to talk myself into going into the church. When the funeral director told us it was time to go in, I looked at Mama and Daddy, and I realized they were having just as hard a time as me. I grasped both of their hands, and together, we walked to the front of the church, where my brother lay surrounded by more flowers than I had ever seen in my life.

When I caught sight of Derrick's face, I lost it. I crumpled to the floor, and I started screaming and yelling. Daddy tried to lift me, but he was torn up, too, and Mama was incoherent. Finally, someone managed to get all three of us seated, and I spent the rest of the service sitting up under Daddy. I stared at my brother a few times, and I actually thought I saw him breathing, but the waxiness of his face told me it was just wishful thinking on my part.

As they closed the casket, someone began singing "It's So Hard to Say Goodbye to Yesterday," and Mama, Daddy and I lost it again, as did most of the congregation. Finally the minister asked the singer to stop the song, and he stood up to deliver his eulogy, none of which I really heard.

Going to the cemetery seemed so final. My brother's body was committed to the ground, and before I realized it, I had thrown myself at the casket. I stood there crying for what seemed like forever. Finally Kyle grabbed me and led me away.

"I told your mom I'd take you back to the house," he said quietly.

I just nodded. We rode in silence for a while until it must have got the best of Kyle and he turned on the radio. We were almost to the house when the song I had recorded with Mocha Love came on. I smiled—until I realized my brother wasn't there to share the joy with me.

I finally snapped off the radio and looked out the window, knowing that my life would never be the same.

Two weeks later, Mama and Daddy both returned to work, but I couldn't bring myself to do anything more than lie in bed. My cell phone was blowing up constantly, but I didn't feel like talking to anyone, so I ignored it. I found myself at least once a day slipping off to sit in Derrick's car, which made me feel so much closer to him. I still couldn't believe he was gone.

Kyle stopped by every day after his classes, which had started a week ago, and most days he didn't even say anything. He just sat with me, ready to listen if I wanted to talk. He even brought his little brother, Tony, over a couple of times, which was about the only time I laughed.

I was just about to grab a bowl of cereal one afternoon when I was waiting for Kyle when the phone rang. I had been ignoring it for the longest, but for some reason, I answered, and the voice I heard on the other end made me groan.

"Where are you?" T asked.

"Why?" I asked with an attitude.

"Look, I know you're probably still mad, but we're supposed to be in the studio today. You need to get down here."

"You really think I'm going into the studio with you?" I asked. "Whatever, T." I hung up the phone just as Kyle walked through the front door with a bag of White Castle hamburgers.

"Hey," he said just as the house phone rang. "You want me to get that?"

I just shrugged. He picked it up and spoke for a few seconds, then handed me the phone.

"Who is it?" I asked.

"Some woman," he said.

I sighed and grabbed the phone. "Hello."

"Hey, Jasmine. It's Jessica from DC Records," she said, sounding more professional than I had ever heard her.

"Hey," I said.

"Please hold a moment for Ron." She didn't even wait for me to respond before she put me on hold.

Ron came on the line a few seconds later. "Jasmine, how have you been?" he asked.

"Not good," I said.

"Yeah, I heard about your brother," Ron said. "I'm real sorry to hear that. Did you guys get the flowers we sent to the funeral?"

"Yes," I said, not knowing if we had or not. "They were really nice. Thank you."

He was silent for a second. "We've left several messages for you. You're supposed to be in the studio today recording. You also missed two other recording sessions, as well as deejaying Teen Scene."

I shook my head, trying to figure out why he was pressing me when he knew my brother had died.

"Look, I can't do it right now," I said. "I've got a lot going on."

"I understand, but business is business. I expect you in the studio this afternoon."

"Whatever," I said, and hung up on him.

Kyle and I sat around watching TV until my parents got home that evening. I said goodbye, then headed to my room, where my cell phone was beeping, indicating that I had a message.

Actually, I had about thirty of them. A few were from friends from school offering their condolences, but there were some about gigs I had lined up that I hadn't shown up for. There were three from T, as well as a few from the guy whose twenty-first birthday I was supposed to deejay. There were also several from both Ron and DC, all of them sounding kind of threatening.

I ignored them all. Just as I was about to turn off my phone, it rang, and without thinking, I answered it.

"It's about time," someone said.

"Who is this?" I asked.

"Oh, so it's like that? You just take my money and then pretend you don't know who I am?"

"Who is this?" I repeated.

"Who do you think it is?"

"Look, I don't have time for games. Either tell me who this is or I'm hanging up."

"It's Jeremy. You were supposed to deejay my twenty-first birthday party two weeks ago."

"Oh," I said. "Look, I'm real sorry. I have some personal stuff going on right now."

"Why is that my problem?" he said. "I looked like a fool. I spent all this money on a party and didn't have a DJ the whole weekend."

"I'll pay you back," I said, getting ready to hang up.

"I know you will," he said. "Even if I have to come over to your house and get it myself."

"You don't know where I live," I said, laughing to myself.

"You wanna bet?" he said, and rattled off my address.

"How'd you know that?" I asked. I had had him send his money to Loretta's house. Then it hit me. "Loretta gave you my address?"

"Yeah," he said. "When I couldn't get in touch with you, I called her. She refused at first, but then I offered her a grand, and she told me."

"Look, I told you I'll get you your money," I said.

"But can you get me back my reputation? People all over Queens are laughing at me. I had to set up a boom box for my party."

The image made me laugh, which only made him angrier.

"Oh, so I'm funny to you? Keep on laughing. I'm going to be someone someday, and when I am, I will ruin you."

"Fine," I said. "I'm already dead anyway."

A week later, Kyle talked me into going to the movies. I really didn't want to go, but he insisted it would be good for me to get out of the house. We went to see some comedy that had me laughing so hard my sides hurt. I felt guilty all the way home for having a good time so soon after my brother was gone.

The next morning, Mama came and woke me up.

"How are you doing?" she asked, stroking my hair.

"Okay," I said.

"I'm glad you went out last night."

I didn't respond, and I guess she saw the guilt on my face, because she said, "Baby, life has to go on. As hard as it might be for us to move forward, we don't have much of a choice. Derrick wouldn't want us to stop living."

A tear slid down my face. "Why'd he leave me, Mama?" I asked, clinging to her.

She started crying, too. "I don't know, baby. I don't know."

"I don't know what I'm feeling. One minute I feel

guilty because I was yelling and screaming at him right before it happened, and the next I'm angry at him for not getting a better car. If he wouldn't have been out there fooling around with it, he would still be here with us."

She stroked my hair. "You can't do this to yourself. Don't beat yourself up, baby."

"But I didn't even get to tell him I loved him," I said, crying harder.

"He knows, baby. He knows."

We sat in silence for a long time, just holding each other. Finally Mama said she was going out for a while, and she asked if I wanted to come, but I wasn't in the mood.

I got up to take a shower, and while I was in the bathroom, I realized I needed to be near my brother. I quickly got dressed and headed to my car, but then I changed my mind and got into Derrick's car and headed to the cemetery.

It was the first time I had been there since my brother had been buried almost a month ago, and it took me a few minutes to find his grave. The marker wasn't in yet, so someone had set up a wooden cross with Derrick's name on it. I sat in the cool dirt and just talked to him for what seemed like hours. It was the best I had felt in weeks.

When I finally looked up, I realized it was starting to get dark, so I headed home.

I went to start Derrick's car, and the engine just sputtered. I couldn't help but laugh. It was like Derrick was playing a joke on me through his stupid car. After a few more tries, the car still wouldn't start, so I called home, happy when Daddy answered.

He promised to come get me, and as I looked around at the cemetery, which seemed to be getting darker by the second, I decided to wait outside the gates. I had seen too many horror movies where bad things happened to people in cemeteries, and I was not trying to be a victim.

It seemed to take Daddy forever, but he finally came and got Derrick's car started. He offered to pick us up something to eat, so after making sure I made it home safely, he drove off.

When I saw Mama's car in the driveway, I couldn't help but smile. I realized she was right: we had to keep on living.

"Mama," I called, walking through the front door. I headed to the den, where I heard the television. "Mama."

She still didn't answer, so I figured she was in the bathroom. I was just about to head toward the back of the house when I noticed Mama sitting in a chair in the corner.

"Hey," I said, stepping into the room.

It took me a second to process that her mouth was covered with duct tape and her hands were tied behind her back.

"Mama," I said, rushing over to her, but before I could make it, a man stepped out of nowhere and pointed a gun at her head.

chapter 17

I just knew I had to be dreaming. I shook myself, praying that I would wake up to find that the last couple of months had been a dream, but when I felt myself being forced onto our sofa so I was facing Mama, I knew this was a nightmare come to life.

"You okay, Mama?" I asked.

"Shut up!" the man yelled.

I quickly did what he said, but I stared at Mama, silently communicating my question.

She nodded, which made me feel a little better.

We sat there in silence for the longest time in the dark, and I tried my best to make out the man's features. Something about him seemed really familiar, but I wasn't sure who he was.

It finally occurred to me that Daddy should be

home any second, which kind of scared me. I didn't want this man hurting my parents.

When I finally heard Daddy's key in the lock, I breathed a sigh of relief. The guy hadn't bothered to tie me up, and I thought about running, but I figured he'd shoot me before I even made it to the door, so I called out instead.

"Daddy, help!" I yelled.

I guess something in my voice let him know I was serious. By the time he made it to the den, the man was standing over me with the gun pointed at my head. For some reason, I wasn't scared. Actually, the thought of seeing my brother again brought me some peace.

Daddy took in the scene pretty quickly and held up his hands.

"Man, you can take whatever you want. Just don't hurt my family," he said, slowly making his way into the room.

The guy just gave this weird laugh and shook his head.

"Your family has been hurting me for years," he said.

That was the most he had said since I had walked into the house, and it finally hit me where I knew the voice from.

"Ron?" I asked.

He quickly looked at me. Realizing his cover was blown, he walked over and switched on the light, then pulled off his black skull cap.

"Chubby?" Daddy said. "Man, what are you doing?"

"What does it look like I'm doing?" he said. "I'm sick and tired of your family messing things up for me."

I looked back and forth from Ron to Daddy. "You know each other?" I asked.

Ron snorted. "I guess you can call it that."

I looked at Mama and saw recognition in her eyes, too.

She tried to say something, but the tape was still covering her mouth.

Ron walked over and snatched it off, and Mama screamed in pain. Daddy took that chance to rush him, and he was able to tackle Ron to the ground and begin punching him. I had never seen Daddy so angry, and I watched in fascination for a few seconds before it occurred to me to call 911.

The operator had just taken my information when Ron managed to flip Daddy over and stand over him with the trigger cocked.

Without thinking, I threw down the phone and raced over. "Why are you doing this?" I yelled.

My question stopped him, and he turned to me. "Because once again the Richardson family is about to mess up my career."

"What are you talking about?" I asked.

"First your mother ruined my career years ago when she talked your daddy out of the deal I set up. Then your brother messed things up when he told you not to sign with DC. I thought I could just get rid of him and that would get you back in line, but no, you still decide you don't want to show up for sessions. Do you know how much money we've lost on you?"

I stared at him, my mouth wide open. "You killed my brother?" I asked softly.

"You're right I killed him, just like I'm about to kill your pathetic parents. You guys make me sick. Your father and I were going to be famous years ago, but your mother had to get pregnant. It's all your brother's fault that I didn't get my record deal."

We all just stood there staring at him, but it was like he didn't see us. He was sweating, and his eyes were wide.

"I hate this family!" he screamed. "I want you all dead. Do you know I'm about to lose my job because of you? If I don't get Jasmine into the studio tonight, I won't have a job tomorrow. Do you know how long I've been working to build my career?" he asked, but none of us bothered to respond. "Do you?

"You know what? I'm just going to have to show you, because you guys think I'm playing with you." He cocked the trigger again and began swinging the gun wildly. Daddy and I backed up, but Mama was still tied to the chair and couldn't move.

Ron swung to face her.

"I can't stand you. You knew I loved you, Pat, and you went ahead and married this fool anyway. You knew how I felt about you. Then you had the nerve to get pregnant by him and have him mess up my career. Now that your son is dead, have you been hurting the way you hurt me?"

Mama just looked at him as tears streamed down her face.

"What have you done?" she finally whispered.

"Yeah, it doesn't feel good, does it?" Ron said, smiling.

"Ron," Mama said, and she looked at the floor like she was searching for the words.

"Patricia," Daddy said in that warning tone he saved for the times when we'd better do what he said.

"No, baby. It's past time he knows," she said.

"Pat, don't you see this man is crazy? That's the reason you didn't tell him then," Daddy said.

A look of calm came over Mama's face. "It's time," she said, just as we heard the police sirens.

"What are you guys talking about?" Ron said.

Mama took a deep breath. "Derrick was your son."

Ron was still stunned as police led him away in handcuffs, but his shock didn't have anything on mine.

After the officers questioned us, we sat around in silence for what seemed like forever. It wasn't until the phone started beeping that I realized it was off the hook, so I replaced it and then turned to Mama.

"Were you ever planning on saying anything?" I asked quietly.

She just shook her head.

"So all this stuff about Daddy quitting the band to take care of you and Derrick, that wasn't true?"

I looked back and forth between my parents, and finally Daddy said, "It's true. I loved your mother long before she hooked up with Chubby. Around the time she found out she was pregnant, we realized Chubby was crazy, and she decided she didn't want to have anything to do with him. When he cheated me out of some money, I knew it was time to go.

Your mother and I talked, and we agreed to get married and raise Derrick together. We didn't want any interference from Chubby—Ron."

I didn't know what to say.

"Look," Daddy said, "as far as I'm concerned, Derrick is my son. I was there from the minute he was born, and I've been there every step of the way. Just because he's not mine biologically doesn't mean anything to me."

"Am I yours?" I asked quietly.

My parents just looked at me.

"What kind of stupid question is that?" Mama asked. "Of course he's your father."

"How am I supposed to know what the truth is anymore?" I shouted. "You guys have been lying to us for years."

"Speaking of lying," Daddy said, "is there something you want to tell us?"

It took me a few seconds to figure out what he was talking about.

"I was going to tell you about the record deal," I said, "but then Derrick was killed, and well, I just never got around to it."

Daddy just took a deep breath and sighed. "How many albums is it for?"

"Five," I said. .

"Are you crazy?" he shouted. "Why would you sign that type of deal?"

"Because they were the only ones offering it," I yelled right back.

Daddy ignored my tone. "What are the terms of the agreement?" he asked, running his hand down his face.

"I'm not sure," I said.

"Where's the contract?"

I tried to remember, but I couldn't, so I shrugged.

"You need to call Henry," Mama said softly.

"Don't worry about it," I said. "I signed the deal, so I'll honor it."

Mama ignored me. "Go call your brother," she said.

Daddy left the room without saying another word.

Mama and I just sat in silence.

"We've made a real mess of things, huh?" she finally said.

I just nodded. Suddenly the events of the past few weeks got to me, and before I knew it, I was crying harder than I had ever cried in my life. Mama grabbed me and held on like she would never let me go, and I realized she was crying, too.

When Daddy came into the room, he took one look at us and grabbed us both.

"We're going to be okay," he said, and I really believed him.

Once we finally settled down, Daddy said Uncle Henry wouldn't be able to come over until the next day, because he had some huge meeting that evening.

I slept in the bed with my parents again that night, and we stayed up talking about Derrick and trying to figure out what the future held.

The next morning when I woke up, the first thing I saw was the television broadcasting a picture of Ron being led to a courthouse.

Apparently, when I had called 911, our whole conversation had been recorded, so they had his confession of killing my brother on tape. The anchor also said that there was evidence that Ron had murdered Lenny the nightclub owner.

I just shook my head in amazement. I had never been so close to someone so evil.

I had just come out of the bathroom when the phone rang.

"Hello," I said.

"You okay?" I couldn't help but smile at Kyle's concern.

"I'm fine," I said. "Yesterday was crazy."

"I'll be right over," he said.

I started to protest, but I realized I really wanted to see him.

By the time Kyle arrived, reporters were standing around in our front yard and our phone was ringing off the hook. Mama and Daddy had decided to take the day off, and we were seriously thinking of un-plugging the phone when it rang again. I glanced at the caller ID and saw T's number, and I answered more out of curiosity than anything.

"Hey," he said. "I'm surprised you answered."

"I'm surprised you called," I said with an attitude.

"Look, I heard about what went down last night and about what Ron did to your brother. I just wanted you to know that I'm really sorry."

"Why would you be sorry?" I asked.

"I feel like I'm partly to blame," he said.

I looked around in confusion, and Kyle glanced at me, silently asking if everything was okay. I nodded.

"Why would you feel like you're to blame?" I asked slowly.

He paused for a minute. "Look, there's no easy way to say this," he said. "The reason I started dating you is because DC asked me to get close to you—"

"What?" I said.

The alarm in my voice sent Kyle to my side.

"DC asked you to date me?"

"Yeah," he said, "but once I got to know you, I really liked you."

"So I was just a game to you?" I said, feeling hurt. "So the way we just clicked, that was just you messing with me?"

"Some of it was real, but most of it was because Loretta gave me some information about you," he admitted.

"Loretta gave you information about me?" I repeated slowly.

"Yeah," he said. "She met DC after that first show you were in, and he promised to help her get her modeling career off the ground if she helped him sign you."

I sat down, stunned. I thought the day before had been full of surprises, but once again I found myself speechless.

"Look, I just wanted you to hear it from me. Loretta and I are going to kick it for a while. I didn't want you to be surprised if you saw pictures of us together."

I laughed under my breath. "So are you just using her, too?"

"Nah," he said quickly. "I've got nothing but love

for her. I mean, she has her flaws, but she's a good person."

"Yeah, she does have her flaws, with her *Finding Nemo* breasts," I said, remembering the fish from the animated movie who had one fin smaller than the other. "You are really going to date a woman who has one breast bigger than the other? Those breast implants are jacked up." I couldn't help but laugh as I remembered walking in on T and seeing Loretta's disproportionate breasts.

"DC's already taken care of that for her," he said.

I hung up the phone and laughed so hard that I started crying. Kyle just stood there looking at me like I was crazy.

"You okay?" he finally asked.

"Man, my life can't get any crazier," I said just as the phone rang again.

I don't know why I answered it, but I immediately regretted that I did.

"Good morning, Jasmine," a chipper female said.

"Jessica?" I asked, realizing it was DC's assistant.

"Yeah. Hold one second for DC."

Before I could respond, T's latest hit was blasting through the phone. Once again curiosity got the best of me, and I waited about thirty seconds before DC came on the line.

"Jasmine," he said, "I'm sorry to hear about what happened at your place last night."

"I just bet you are," I said.

"I don't know what possessed Ron to act the way he did. I want you to know that this is no reflection on DC Records. When can we get you in the studio?"

I thought about my promise to hold up my end of the contract, and I realized it wasn't worth it. I'd already lost my brother, I'd almost lost my parents and, just like Derrick had told me, I was selling my soul to the devil if I recorded with DC.

"I'll have to talk to my attorney," I said.

"About what?" DC said. "You signed a contract. We have a deal."

I knew he was right, but I still wanted to try and get out of it. "I'll have my attorney call you," I said, and hung up.

I spent the rest of the day trying to figure out what I had done with the contract. Uncle Henry had called and said he would be over later that evening and that he'd like to see a copy of it.

Kyle and I looked for hours, but I couldn't find it. By the time he left that evening, I was beyond frustrated, and I found myself getting mad at my brother. When I lost things, he was always the one who told me where they could be found. I realized just how much I missed him. I walked into his room and looked around. Everything was just as he had left it. A few boxes were packed with the stuff he'd been planning to take to school with him. I looked at it and felt my eyes filling with tears, knowing his dreams of becoming a doctor would never be fulfilled.

I glanced around and spotted the framed newspaper article from the night we had won All-District. We both looked so happy.

"I miss you, Derrick," I said. "You always had my back. What am I supposed to do without you?" I sat waiting for him to answer, but no answer came.

Finally I decided to go sit in his car for a while. It always made me feel closer to him. I got in and turned on the radio and just sat there chilling, thinking about my brother and all that had happened since the beginning of the summer. When I thought about the day he died, the tears came. I had said such horrible things to him, when all he was trying to do was protect me.

I realized he'd been right. I had been acting like a witch. I thought about all the money I had made and how it had caused me to disrespect my parents, my brother and most of all myself, and I just cried harder. I didn't like the person I had become. I had totally gotten away from my love of music just to chase the money, and that wasn't cool at all.

I reached into the backseat for the box of tissues Derrick kept there and ended up feeling up under the seat for it. I was just about to give up when I felt it. I grabbed the wad and realized it wasn't the tissue.

My heart started thudding as it hit me what I held in my hands. Even in death, my brother was helping me out. He had led me right to the contract.

I didn't know whether to laugh or cry. I hurried to my room to make sure my eyes weren't deceiving me, and they weren't.

I had never been so glad to see a stack of paper in my life.

When Uncle Henry arrived, it hardly took him a minute to look through the contract.

"Who signed this?" he asked when he got to the final page and glanced at the signature.

"I did," I said.

"Were your parents there with you?" he asked, looking at Mama and Daddy for confirmation.

"No," I said.

He laughed.

"This agreement isn't binding," he said, tossing it aside. "You're a minor. You can't sign a contract."

"So I don't have to record the albums?" I asked.

"Not one line," he said, turning to Daddy. "You would have known this if you'd finished school. This is basic stuff."

Daddy looked like he was about to go off, so I quickly said, "So what do I tell DC?"

"Nothing," Uncle Henry said. "I'll deal with him."

I just nodded. "So I don't have a record deal?" I said. The thought actually made me kind of sad.

Uncle Henry looked at me, and his face softened. "Not this time, but that doesn't mean you can't get one."

"You know, you can still go to school if you want," Mama said. "I'm sure under the circumstances we can talk to some people and get you in somewhere."

"I guess," I said. "I really haven't thought much about college since I decided not to go. I was planning to pursue my music, you know."

"I know," Mama said, and for the first time, I felt like she really did. "You're only sixteen. You have your whole life ahead of you. Why don't you take a few months and decide what you want to do? Didn't I hear you and Kyle talking about doing an album yourselves? You can work on that for the next few months, and if it doesn't work out, you can start school in the spring."

I thought about what she said and nodded. "Thank you," I said, standing up and giving her a hug.

"For what?" she asked.

"For not killing my dreams."

epilogue

Three years later

I stood backstage at the Beacon Theater in Manhattan, taking deep breaths. In all the years I had been onstage, I could never remember being so nervous. Despite my nerves, I knew I was going to be fine.

"Hey, beautiful," Kyle said, coming up behind me with a dozen roses. He gave me a kiss, and I couldn't help but smile at the tingle that ran down my spine.

"Hey, baby," I said.

"You ready?" he asked.

"As ready as I'll ever be," I said.

All around us people were hustling, getting ready for that night's event.

"Are my parents here?"

"Now, you know not to even ask that. Your daddy has two digital cameras and a video camera. He and your mom are sitting in the front row."

I went and peeped out from behind the curtain and spotted my parents. Mama must have felt me looking at them, because she turned my way and waved before nudging Daddy, who immediately began taking pictures. I blew them both a kiss and then headed back over to Kyle.

"Do I look okay?" I asked, straightening my clothes.

"You look fantastic," he said.

Suddenly I heard the music start, and Kyle leaned over and gave me another kiss. "That's from me for good luck," he said before planting another one on my cheek. "That's from Tony," he said.

"Oh, why does the kiss from your brother have to be on my cheek?" I joked.

"Because no one touches those lips but me," he said, and grinned.

I just laughed.

"I'll see you later," he said. "I love you."

"I love you, too," I said.

As people began making their way onstage, I stood back and watched in awe. I had been working my butt off for the last three years, going to school year round, to make my dreams come true, and I had pictured this moment in my head so many times. I couldn't help but smile. I was actually living my dream.

Someone touched me and indicated it was time for me to make my way onstage. I smiled my thanks, straightened my outfit one more time and stepped from behind the curtain to deafening applause. The spotlight almost blinded me, but I had practiced walking to the stage so many times that I didn't need to see where I was going to make it to the center.

I grabbed the microphone as the crowd quieted down. Just as I was about to speak, someone screamed out, "I love you, Jasmine." I knew it was Kyle, and I grinned.

"I love you, too," I yelled. I looked at the people behind me. "Y'all ready to do this?" I asked, and they nodded.

I turned back to face the audience.

"Good evening," I said, "and welcome to NYU's 2010 graduation. My name is Jasmine Richardson, and I am your valedictorian."

The applause started up again. After it died down, I began my speech.

"Three years ago, like many of you, I was un-decided about what I wanted to do with my life. My brother, Derrick, had recently been killed, and I just knew I wanted a career in music. It wasn't until I signed a crazy contract with DC Records, which is now out of business, thank God, that I realized that I wasn't as smart as I thought. I realized that there are a lot of people who want to be the next big thing, and while there's nothing wrong with that, I also realized that we need people behind the scenes who have others' best interests at heart.

"I've been working for the last three years, going to school year-round, to do my part to make that happen. For many of you, the real world begins tomorrow, but for me, I have three more years of law school."

There was a loud round of applause.

"I don't want you to count me out of the music game just yet, either. Most of y'all have seen me around campus, deejaying at parties and singing at different functions. What many of you don't know is that I've also been busy working on my first album, which hits stores in a couple of weeks.

"Some of you are probably wondering what this has to do with you. Actually, more than you think. I said all this to say that wherever life takes you, always remember to follow your dreams and to do what makes you happy. Even if no one else believes in you, believe in yourself. Good night and God bless."

READING GROUP GUIDE

1. Jasmine's passion was music and Loretta's passion was modeling. What is your greatest passion to pursue and why?

2. Jasmine's brother, Derrick, was her best friend. Discuss ways Derrick's death affected Jasmine. How does it feel to lose someone close to you—whether it's through death or just the ending of a relationship?

3. Jasmine was covaledictorian of her class, and she was skipped. Describe how Jasmine showed book sense but not common sense.

4. Ron/Chubby held a grudge for almost twenty years. List grudges you've held against people and how you've let go of them.

5. Jasmine was torn between her feelings for Kyle and her feelings for Triple T. Why do you think Jasmine was attracted to Triple T? How does it feel to like more than one person at the same time, and how do you decide whom you want to be with?

6. Jasmine's parents were not supportive of her musical aspirations. How did they show they weren't supportive? How does it feel to not have

the support of those close to you when there is something you really want to do?

7. Loretta was not pleased with her appearance, so she got a boob job. If you had the chance to change anything about your appearance, what would it be, and why?

8. DC had a reputation for dealing with gangsta rappers and not being a nice person. How important is your reputation to you, and why?

9. Jasmine was very hurt when she learned Loretta had cheated on her with Triple T. How would you handle the situation if you discovered your boyfriend/girlfriend was cheating on you with your best friend?

10. Jasmine got tired of her parents' rules, so she moved out. If you moved out of your parents' house today, where would you go and what would you do to support yourself?

TEXT ME LIST

Favorite female artist: Mary J. Blige

Favorite male artist: Luther Vandross

Favorite actress: Regina King

Favorite actor: Denzel Washington

Favorite comedian: Bernie Mac

Favorite movie: *The Five Heartbeats*

Favorite romantic movie: *The Notebook*

Favorite online site: www.chandrasparkstaylor.com

Favorite song: "Adore" by Prince

Favorite book: The Bible

Favorite meal: Grilled chicken, white rice and broccoli

People I most admire: My parents, Cedric L. Sparks and Doris Jones Sparks

Favorite city to visit: Birmingham, Alabama

Favorite day of the week: Sunday

3567405265960S